BROKEN BRANCHES

ALSO BY THIS AUTHOR

THE RADIO

THE PAGE

A TINY FEELING OF FEAR

BROKEN BRANCHES

M. JONATHAN LEE

This paperback edition published | 2017

First published | 2017
1 2 3 4 5 6 7 8 9 10

Hideaway Fall publishing
BBIC S75 1JL UK
www.hideawayfall.com

ISBN | 978-0-9954923-3-2
Copyright © M Jonathan Lee 2017

A catalogue copy of this book is available from the British Library.

Set in Century Schoolbook MT

Lyrics reproduced by kind permission of Pinegrove © ASCAP 2016 Run For Cover Records, LLC | Original art by Terry Brookes | 2016

Printed and bound by Charlesworth Press | 2017

Visit www.jonathanleeauthor.com | www.hideawayfall.com

For Grandpa

"The truth is I lost all track of time
And I wound up wandering
Unraveling fragments all inside
But I rise up all aligning"

- Pinegrove

ONE

More than a hundred years had passed since the single tiny seed broke free and left its home. All alone, it took its first and final flight. It spun happily on the wind, powerless as to its destination, carried over the butterscotch fields. It climbed and fell and rotated and danced on the breeze until, finally, the time came for it to descend into the long blades of grass below.

Its first journey was over.

A second was about to begin.

And now, it seemed as if the sycamore tree had evolved. No longer just a tree, it was something altogether more powerful, something that controlled everything around it, right down to the wind, the sun and the rain. And the occupants of Cobweb Cottage, who slept restlessly a few metres above its thick roots.

Ian Perkins could tell you of its power. He should know. He had spent most of his life in its shadow.

Ian was sitting on the box seat by the lounge window. From here he could see the full expanse of square lawn that ended at the white wooden fence far in the distance. The fence continued to a right angle, where it switched direction and followed the garden until it disappeared down past the side of the house. To some extent the boundary was pointless; Ian's nearest neighbours were more than four miles away over the sweeping fields. On a clear winter day it was just possible to see the smoke escaping their chimney in the distance. Sometimes the smoke was the only indication that the world around him was still inhabited.

At the top of the garden, on the other side of the fence, the land fell away into a ditch. A small stream ran along the bottom. In the heavy rains that often hit this area of the country, the stream would overflow and muddy water would creep up and under the fence, threatening to swallow the lawn. The road that led away from this forsaken place ran parallel with the stream.

Cobweb Cottage sat at the end of that road.

In years gone by, the road had been a simple thoroughfare. Passing wagons and horses would continue along the well-worn track past the cottage to the east, to sell their wares in the nearby village. That was until Ian's great-great-grandfather claimed the land and blocked the thoroughfare. Nowadays, you had to be coming specifically to Cobweb Cottage to find yourself there.

Ian inspected the lawn. Beneath the morning dew he could just make out the lines in the grass. Two different shades of silvery blue. Dark and light. He had spent all of the previous day pushing the lawnmower up and down the huge expanse of grass. His eyes followed the lines to the left. He was happy: they ran perfectly parallel to the drive. But off to the right, where they reached the centre of the garden, he saw they began to curve, sweeping dramatically around the huge sycamore tree that stood directly in front of the cottage. Spreading from its trunk was a large circle of roots and soil where nothing else could grow. The tree's trunk was almost as wide as the window at which Ian was sitting. He hated the tree. It had brought so much suffering, so much misery, on the family.

The tree had frightened Ian ever since he was a young child. Unfortunately, the window of his childhood bedroom had looked out from the front of the cottage. In those days, the tree had reminded him of an upturned witch's broom. The trunk was the handle. Thick individual branches tapered high above, threatening to sweep away the yawning sky. There were many nights where the moon cast shadows on the wall above his bed and the tree's branches – like fingers – silently scraped and scratched the wallpaper above him. On those nights, he would plant his face directly into the pillow and gently sob, careful that his father didn't hear him in the room below.

Even back then, the tree must have been more than a hundred years old. Now, thirty (or so) years later, the tree had taken on a different, more ominous look. In those intervening years, it seemed to have doubled in size. The branches now fanned out like peacock feathers, casting an endless darkness over the cottage. The trunk was much wider, swallowing up more of the garden as it grew. You could still see the remains of the treehouse Ian had built high up in the tree.

The tree eclipsed the cottage. In the right light, somewhere around dusk, it was possible to persuade yourself (if you took the time to study it for long enough) that it was more than a tree. The shapes in its thick bark formed eyes; the giant knot

11

beneath, a mouth – within which split wood formed sharp teeth. And at times its branches, separating down the middle, swaying together, formed fingers and hands and arms. Yes, it was more: a huge monster standing guard, taking ownership of the cottage and its occupants. There was no escape from it now. It was pushing its giant roots out of the earth ready, it seemed, to take three giant paces forward and stamp the cottage into the ground.

As Ian stared, his eyes were drawn to the thickest of all the branches. It formed a perfect right angle with the trunk, and pointed directly at him. He couldn't recall a time when a tiny burst of shoots or leaves had appeared on the branch. In all seasons, it remained withered and bare, stretching accusingly at the cottage like an arthritic finger. In the summertime, as the rest of the tree flourished, the surface would slowly begin to peel from this branch. Within a matter of days the entire bark would be shed, like a snakeskin, lying across the exposed roots on the hard ground below.

Two small hooks were just visible in the branch, slowly being devoured by the tree as each year passed. Ian remembered the bright summer morning that his father had climbed his ladder and secured the hooks. Beneath them he'd attached two thick cords of blue rope, which disappeared through the varnished yellow seat and reappeared as thick knots below. Ian, and his older brother Stuart, had spent many summer days laughing as they swung beneath the creaking, twisted branch, the horizon turning from green to blue and back again. They would take it in turns to leap from the swing, the other carefully marking the landing place with a plant pot. There was something vitally important in knowing who had jumped the furthest, who had won. Invariably, it was Stuart. Ian used to complain that he had the disadvantage of having much shorter legs. Stuart would argue that Ian was lighter and therefore would fly further. Usually, the argument would end in laughter, with the two boys collapsed in the rough dirt in the shade of the trunk.

But that was many years ago, back in a time where life seemed colourful and bright. Long before the morning that Stuart had awoken, walked over to the barn at the back of the cottage, loaded his shotgun and blasted his head off.

And thus, as simple as that, the curse had wound its way down another generation of the Perkins family tree.

Calmly claiming its next victim.

From just outside the door that led to the hall, Ian heard little footsteps padding softly down the stairs. He quickly wiped the tears from his eyes and turned to see small pink fingers appearing around the edge of the door frame.

TWO

"Hello, Daddy. It's a good morning." Harry stood with his back against the door. He was smiling, apparently pleased with his observation.

"It certainly is, Harry." Ian dragged his pyjama sleeve across his eyes. Just in case.

"Daddy okay?"

"Daddy's fine. How are you today?"

"I'm great!"

With that, Harry left his position against the door and tore across the room to where Ian was standing. As he got closer, he outstretched his arms, popping open two of the press studs that ran down the front of his red pyjamas. Ian collected him and swept him up into his chest. He held Harry's head in his palm and tightly pulled their bodies together as closely as possible. He breathed in the smell of strawberry from Harry's hair.

Harry coughed dramatically, as if he was suffocating, and attempted to release himself from Ian's hug. Ian lifted Harry up in front of him. His brown wavy hair was stuck to the side of his face, suggesting he had slept soundly. Ian stared into his eyes, taking in the different shades of brown that swirled around his black pupils. Ian smiled. There was no way of even beginning to express the love he felt for his son. In the situation he currently found himself in, he had no idea what he would have done without his only son. It didn't bear thinking about.

In what appeared to be a purposeful act of sabotage, the tree's branches swayed, allowing a blast of early morning sunlight through. Harry squinted.

Ian pulled him back into his chest.

He didn't want to let him go.

Ever.

Harry struggled to break free again and Ian gently lowered him onto the arm of the sofa. There, he was at Ian's shoulder height. Ian kept one arm around his waist.

"Well, we'd better get you some breakfast, hadn't we, little man?"

Harry pulled a face that suggested Ian had said the stupidest thing he had ever heard.

"Er, no, Daddy. I'm big now."

Ian chuckled.

"Don't you remember, Daddy? I'm four now. Ef. Oh. Ar. Four."

"Okay," Ian said, smiling. "Do you want to get down?"

"Daddy, I can do it."

Harry gave a look that reminded Ian of his wife. A warning.

Before Harry could move, Ian scooped him up, spun him upside down above his head and placed him feet first on the floor. Realising his sudden freedom, Harry took three quick steps forward, then stopped abruptly and turned around. He held up a small, podgy finger and narrowed his eyes.

"No," he said, "you wait here."

Ian motioned forwards.

Harry screamed excitedly and set off running down the length of the lounge toward the kitchen.

"I'm coming for you!"

"Oh no!" laughed Harry as he disappeared around the corner. "Oh no!"

THREE

Unfortunately, Rachel didn't share the early morning happy-to-be-alive enthusiasm with which Harry had greeted Ian. After Harry had left for the day, Rachel finally made her way downstairs. Her journey from the box bedroom at the end of the landing, down the stairs, along the hall and into the kitchen seemed to get longer each day. Her whole body ached and her feet were heavy to lift. Every single step was an effort. On some days she didn't even bother to go downstairs. Instead, she stayed in bed, leaving the bathroom as the only other room to visit.

During waking hours, her constant headache never left. Sometimes she wished she'd drunk a bottle of Merlot or two the night before. At least then there'd be a justification for this feeling.

When she finally made it through the hall, Ian was sitting in the kitchen in his chair at the far end of the long range table. As usual, he was staring out of the French doors that opened onto the large back garden. He didn't look up as she walked into the room. His eyes remained transfixed by something in the distance. Something unknown.

Rachel walked across the kitchen tiles; they were cold on her bare feet. She filled the kettle and flicked the switch. Then she stood, all her weight on her right leg, and rubbed her face, trying to waken some life in herself. When that didn't work, she rested her elbows on the work surface and held her face in both hands. How was she going to make it through yet another day of this?

Another day of not dressing.

Another day of not cleaning herself.

Another day of drifting from room to room in a constant haze, surrounded by the dense fog that seemed to override all her senses.

For many weeks, she had felt as if she was wearing a thick woollen hat. She couldn't hear correctly; words were not getting through to her. Everything was fuzzy. And recently, she'd felt like she could no longer speak. There didn't seem to be much point. She could barely form the words in her mind. Pushing them into her throat and then out of her mouth was near impossible. And anyway, by the time she had thought of how to respond, the moment had either passed or she had forgotten the question she had been asked. She couldn't bear to see Ian staring at her with his dark eyes, impatient for an answer. In truth, she couldn't bear to see his face.

When Ian was sure that Rachel wasn't looking, he glanced over in her direction. He could just see the outline of her back around the corner from where he was sitting. Her pink pyjama top had ridden up slightly and he could see the small black bird tattooed at the base of her spine. He recalled the day she had got it.

It was their first holiday alone after Harry was born. After nine months of pregnancy and another year and a half of nappy changing and sleep deprivation, they had finally managed to escape for a long weekend in Portugal. It had taken a few tentative telephone calls before Rachel had managed to persuade her mother to take care of Harry. As soon as she had agreed, Rachel wasted no time finding a hotel and cheap flights online. Within three weeks they were on their way. Ian remembered the feeling as they reached the airport that morning. It was as if life had just begun all over again.

They spent the most part of their long weekend away on the beach, enjoying the freedom to do absolutely nothing. For three days they lay in the baking sun, their hands rarely apart, from just after breakfast to when the man arrived to stack up the sunbeds they'd hired. Everything suddenly felt new and somehow real again.

The tattoo had been a culmination of childlike excitement and a little too much sangria. After a late breakfast on the penultimate morning, Rachel watered the seed she had planted the night before over dinner, that she may like a tattoo.

"That one looks good, Ian," she said, sitting up on her sunbed and pointing at a painfully slim woman at the ocean's edge.

Ian sat up and lifted his sunglasses.

"Over there, in the black bikini bottoms." Rachel pointed.

"The black tattoo? On her shoulder?"

"Yep. I like it."

"Are you serious? It's a bit…"

"Big? Yeah, you might be right actually," she said, laughing. She looked around the beach. It was beginning to fill up. She smiled at Ian, a cheeky smile, and rested her hand on his inner thigh.

"You wouldn't really get one, would you?" Ian said. He recalled her mother had made it clear that she disapproved of the sudden explosion of tattoos on celebrities and footballers worldwide.

"Y'know what? I think I would. I mean, why not?"

"Er…" Ian dragged out the word on purpose.

"My mother? Who cares?" Rachel laughed. "We are in our thirties, after all." Her bravery deserted her for a moment. "Well, she wouldn't need to know."

The conversation continued for the remainder of the day. They spent the afternoon kissing, sleeping and swimming in the sea, but predominantly on the alert for a design that might be the one for Rachel. Ian took great pleasure in waking Rachel to point out the most inappropriate of tattoos. She made it quite clear she didn't want a unicorn, nor the Glasgow Rangers badge.

As the sun became a semi-circle, Rachel shook their towels and began to pack the bags. It was time for them to return to the hotel and prepare for their final evening together, before Harry would remind them that they were parents. Rachel watched as Ian returned from his second journey to the bin. He couldn't have carried all the bottles of San Miguel they had enjoyed over the afternoon in one trip. They left the beach and decided that a glass of sangria was necessary to dispense with the dry taste of beer. One glass became a jug, and one jug became two.

Three hours later, Rachel had an ink-black bird on the base of her spine, halfway inside her pants and halfway out. The bird was in open flight and carried a key in its mouth. Ian had a large red star on his lower arm. He wasn't sure why; it had just seemed like a good idea at the time. They were having such a good time, he didn't want to spoil it by not joining in. Rachel had told him on several occasions that she wouldn't be brave enough to get one if he didn't.

And so he did.

For her.

A blast of steam from the kettle forced Rachel to stand upright, and the little black bird disappeared beneath her pyjama top again. She opened the cupboard door and reached in for a mug. Her movement was slow. Almost robotic. She misjudged the distance from the cupboard to the work surface and the mug clattered down heavily. The sudden noise broke the shell that seemed to be surrounding her thoughts, and her first reaction was to let go of the mug, which fell a short distance on to the granite surface and spun happily, making a pleasant whirring sound before coming to rest, undamaged.

She stood and stared at the mug. Her expression suggested she was trying to understand what had just happened. After a few moments, she raised her eyebrows and then removed the lid from the glass coffee jar and mechanically spooned coffee into the mug. She did the same with the sugar jar and added two sugars. Her hand began to shake as she lifted the kettle. The boiling water sloshed from side to side before finally escaping from the spout and falling onto her hand.

"Fuck," she said. She slammed the kettle down on the side; it slid across the smooth surface and collided with the glass jars.

"You okay?" Ian said.

Rachel ran cold water from the tap onto her hand. Ian got up from the table and stood alongside her. He repeated his question. Silence. He turned and finished making Rachel's drink, making himself one at the same time, then replaced the kettle and straightened the jars so they stood in a straight line again. Labels facing out. He took his mug back to the range table.

The kitchen was like one out of a magazine, the sort that people who like kitchens would cut out and keep. Perhaps beneath a magnet on their fridge, or in a drawer, to secretly retrieve and look at like a lost friend when drinking morning coffee. One that they could only dream about sitting in, never mind owning.

The kitchen was large and wide, the cupboards white and glossy – the type with no handles and, confusingly, you push them in to get them to open out. There were clever storage areas, an eight-hot-plate hob, a wine-cooling cupboard and built-in iPod dock. There was even a television that pulled down from underneath a cupboard like a car's sun visor. It was perfect. Even the floor was heated, though it seemed to have a mind of its own, refusing to work on the coldest of wintery mornings and heating to the temperature of desert sand in the summer. Ian had been known to put on his shoes to cross to the sink to avoid his feet being burned.

Neither Ian nor Rachel had enquired as to how to operate the underfloor heating. Stuart's wife had moved out of the family home a matter of weeks after the incident that distributed her husband's skull around the barn. The cottage was held in a trust set up many years before by one of the Perkins family. On the death of Stuart, the property simply defaulted to the next in line in the family: Ian. At that time, as Stuart's wife cleared the last of her belongings, it seemed entirely inappropriate to ask why sometimes the tiles got warm on their own.

The long range table, where Ian was sitting, matched the cupboards. It looked a little like a boardroom table in some expensive city office: a beautiful long piece of white sheened plastic, with seating for ten. Most of the chairs had never been used, certainly not since Ian and Rachel moved in. Since the incident, Ian hadn't been able to focus properly and he found that hours passed with no discernible memory of what he saw or thought. Each morning he would take the same place at the table and just, well, watch. For the most part he didn't really see what was in front on him; the view outside merging to no more than colours and fuzzy shapes. He would remain focused on the same place until his eyes stung, then he would wipe them and begin his stare again, his mind vacant. From time to time, something in the distance would draw him back to life. Today, it was a magpie. He saw the smudge of its black wings over the woodland and watched as the magpie landed on the arm of a scarecrow in the distance. The irony wasn't lost on him.

Rachel sat at the far end of the table: the chairman of the board. She leafed through a magazine, sipping her coffee from time to time. The room was silent. Somewhere in the distance the vague sound of a tractor could be heard. Neither Rachel nor Ian heard it.

All was quiet.

It was a day much like yesterday and the same as tomorrow.

FOUR

The sun beat down on the cottage, an angry ball of fire relentlessly threatening to melt everything. It seemed to have been this way all summer. Ian was seven years old, Stuart nine. They sat with their backs against the old tree in the front garden, shading themselves from the heat. They had spent the last ten minutes imagining that anything outside of the shade was molten lava. They were surrounded, and they could only watch as the lava flowed slowly past them. Bubbling and popping. Rising by the minute. Getting ever closer.

They were adventurers. And they were trapped. They had to work out a way to escape from beneath the tree. Dust and dirt mingled with the sweat that ran through their hair and down their necks. Four scuffed knees faced the sky, dried blood testifying that they had attempted to get up the tree. Both were panting.

"I'm thirsty," Stuart said.

"Me too."

"Get me a drink, Ian."

"Nah. You get me one."

"Go on."

"Why should I?"

"'Cos I'm thirsty."

"So am I."

"'Cos I'm older than you," Stuart said, attempting an authoritarian tone. It was lost on Ian.

"So?"

"So, you have to do what I say."

Ian smiled. "Yeah, right."

He leaned into his brother and their heads touched, dust and dirt transferring from one brother to another. Stuart had an idea.

"Hey, Ian," he said, suddenly sitting upright, "what if you had, like, special lava shoes, and could only go on the lava for, like, twenty seconds..."

Ian turned to his brother. This sounded interesting.

"...and I'll time how long your lava shoes last and you have a mission."

"What mission?" Ian said excitedly.

"You have to bring the crew special water that recharges them so they can walk on lava."

"The crew?"

"Yeah. It means me and you."

Ian looked puzzled.

"The crew is me and you. Like a crew on a spaceship. Yeah?"

Ian wasn't sure.

"So," repeated Stuart, "you've been, like, issued with special lava shoes to rescue us."

"So-so-so," Ian stuttered excitedly, "like, I'll be one who save-saves the crew? Like, I'll be the hero?"

"Yeah, you'd definitely be the hero. That is..."

26

"What?"

"If you dare to do it."

"I have to dare," said Ian, his eyes wide. "It'll save the crew."

"You need two glasses, full of water," Stuart said.

"Okay," said Ian. He took a deep breath. This was serious. The crew were depending on him.

Stuart began counting as Ian scrambled to his feet.

"And don't spill any – the crew needs it all," Stuart shouted as Ian raced down the garden.

"I won't," Ian shouted over his shoulder.

The two boys gulped down the water as if the glasses may just vanish from their hands at any moment. Ian wiped his hand across his mouth and made a loud aah sound. He had seen somebody do that on television. He was sure that his feet felt different. Somehow fireproof.

"Are the crew safe now?" he said, turning to Stuart.

"They are," he said, placing his arm around his brother. "Thanks to you."

Their heads turned at the same time to find the source of a sound coming from the other side of the tree. It was a car. This was unusual. Apart from their father and a delivery now and again, cars didn't really come around here. The boys squinted in the sunlight as the red car slowly crawled past the white fence and then finally into the mouth of the drive. Ian wondered whether the driver was just going to use the drive to turn around. Now and again somebody would take a wrong turn from the main road and have to travel all the way to the cottage to correct their error. The drive was the only place wide enough along the track to do this.

But not on this occasion. The car edged into the drive and came to a stop just behind their father's tractor. Ian heard the engine clunk to a stop, seemingly relieved to rest. The fan continued to whir. Ian couldn't see the car from where he was sitting, but he heard the definite click of the car lock. The door creaked as it opened. Then he heard it thud shut.

Ian craned his neck. In the bright sunlight it was difficult to make out the figure approaching them. It was definitely a man. He wore jeans and a checked shirt. He had dark hair and sunglasses. Ian watched as the man walked slowly past the tractor, along the drive toward them.

The boys turned to one another. Ian raised his eyebrows; Stuart shrugged. They looked back at the man. He had seen them. He smiled broadly and stepped over the small flowerbed onto the lawn. Ian pulled his knees up closer to him. The lava didn't seem to be affecting the man at all, his shiny brown shoes treading a less than perilous journey toward them. The man removed his sunglasses, cleared his throat and crouched down in front of them. His knees cracked.

"Hey, boys," he said.

Silence.

The man laughed. His teeth were brown, the ends spiralling in yellow and cream fossil shapes. They reminded Ian of aniseed rock.

"You don't remember me, do you?"

Ian shook his head. He shuffled slightly closer to Stuart, hoping his brother would handle this situation.

"Serious?" said the man, wiping the sweat from the hair around his slightly silvered temples.

"Who are you?" said Stuart, attempting the same authoritarian tone he had used earlier. Ian glanced toward the cottage, hoping to see his mother or father in one of the windows.

The man motioned with his finger, and with a shaking hand Ian passed over his half-empty glass. The man threw back the slightly warm liquid in one gulp. He burped and passed the glass back.

"I'm your uncle," he said.

Ian looked at Stuart for confirmation. His back was beginning to get sore from pushing backwards into the trunk of the tree. Stuart's eyes narrowed.

"I am." The man was smiling. "Seriously. I'm your uncle, Stephen."

He held out his hand to shake. Neither of the boys moved.

A voice came from the direction of the cottage.

"What are you doing here?" A simple, direct question.

All three heads turned. Ian was relieved to see his father standing just outside the front door.

Uncle Stephen rose to his feet. His knees cracked again as he did.

"Hello, brother," he said. "How are you?"

29

"I'm okay, thank you."

"Good. Lovely sunny day."

"What do you want, Stephen?"

"I need to talk with you, dear brother. It's urgent."

Uncle Stephen took a pace toward the house.

The boys relaxed slightly. Ian arched his back. He was pleased to remove it from the hard bark of the tree.

"You'd better come inside then."

"Thanks," said Stephen. "A cold drink would be good as well." He turned to the boys. "Hey, don't be sitting under that tree for too long," he whispered, smiling. "You do know it's cursed, right?"

Then he walked toward the house, and for the first time Ian noticed his limp. It was only slight. Perhaps the lava immunity had worn off on his right side.

The two men disappeared inside the house, leaving the front door open behind them.

FIVE

It was just after half past eleven when Ian finally decided to leave the kitchen. He had attempted conversation with Rachel several times and her monotone responses had left an uneasy, almost heavy atmosphere in the room. It felt as if the kitchen was shrinking around him, that there was less air in the room. The silence stretched the room like taut elastic, and he was worried that one more comment would cause Rachel to snap. He couldn't tolerate it anymore. He stood and slid his chair under the table and left the room without speaking.

He quietly pushed open the study door. The room at the bottom of the stairs was now officially the study, but since they'd moved into the cottage a year earlier, the room had already had two prior uses.

When they first arrived, the room had been empty. There were a few boxes scattered here and there and a row of shoes, but nothing more. Rachel had quickly commandeered the room, deciding that it would be perfect as a gym. In the two-bedroomed semi-detached house they had arrived from there was no possibility of such luxuries. Excitedly, she had painted the walls white and covered one with floor-to-ceiling plastic mirrors. On another wall she mounted a television, and opposite there was just enough room for a treadmill, a rowing machine and a small sofa. After only a few weeks, it had become clear that the latter would be the most used of the recent acquisitions.

Predictably, the room's life as an active gym was short-lived. Rachel found it easier to tackle her weight gain with bigger clothes rather than spend time on the dusty treadmill. It had taken Ian a few months to finally prise the key from Rachel and get her to admit that the gym was pretty much a white elephant.

From the moment she allowed Ian to move the gym equipment into the barn, Rachel lost interest in the room altogether. It was now Ian's turn, and it was to become his studio. He painted the walls grey and took down the mirrors. In their place he hung framed posters of The Beatles and Wilco. In came Ian's guitars and his grandmother's old upright piano from the dining room.

Ian took his studio seriously. It was to be his saviour. This was where he was going to write the album that had been swimming around his head for the last twenty years. He had always believed that he would somehow go down a musical path. The problem was that he couldn't play the instruments with any particular dynamism.

In his early teens, he had been taught on the very same piano that now sat in his studio. He made it to grade three, then quickly became disillusioned playing classical pieces and gave up. His grandma on his mother's side pushed him to play for her, but there was something unnerving about the way she insisted on sitting on the stool right alongside him. He could smell her stale breath as she jerked her head from side to side while he played each note, her eyes tightly shut, her tight grey bun loosening as she moved. Sometimes she would continue humming an imaginary tune well after he had finished, whilst he backed quietly out of the room.

In the last few years he had decided that perhaps guitar was more for him. Most of the music he admired was guitar driven, and the hundreds upon hundreds of records that lined the walls of the studio were testament to that. For a number of weeks after he opened his studio in the previous autumn, he would watch guitar lessons online, playing along with them, learning the basic chords one by one. Concentrating his mind brought some comfort.

It was clear that he and Rachel both needed interests apart. Whenever they were together the conversation always drifted to the incident, and when there were no words left to say, the conversation evaporated like frost in the morning sun.

From time to time, Ian would invite Rachel in and play her the opening chords of something he had learned. She would never enter the room completely, instead just lean against the door frame, her unbrushed blond hair hanging over half of her face.

"Did you get it?" Ian would say, after finishing the thirty-second intro he had learned.

Her brow would crinkle, as if she was trying to recall the tune that she hadn't heard.

"No?" Ian would coax. "Come on, you know it."

Rachel would shake her head slowly, her bottom lip covering

33

her top. Ian would then reveal the name of the song and begin to play it again, inviting Rachel to remember. She would manage an expression of vague recollection and then turn and leave, pushing the door closed behind her.

This continued for a month or so, until Ian realised that the six chords he knew were the easiest of all the chords. He would hear a tune and eagerly flick through his music books to find out how to play it. His eyes would scan the necessary chords and his heart would sink if there was an F or, worse still, a B flat.

The guitars began to gather the same amount of dust as the treadmill. The dream of a career on stage was shelved. For the time being at least.

And now, the room was the study. The walls remained grey, the guitars replaced by a desk. Ian eyed the room warily before he entered. Strange things had been happening in the study recently. He scanned the shelves. It was unlikely that any of the records had been touched. He couldn't recall the last time Rachel had entered the study and Harry wasn't tall enough to reach them.

To his left was the old mahogany piano. It was currently utilised for storage. Every available surface was covered with pile after pile after pile of papers. The first few consisted of bills, letters and envelopes (some empty; some unopened). Next to them was a pile of unread magazines and newspaper clippings. After that, and along the lid which covered the piano keys, was Ian's research. This took up the most room.

Since the incident Ian had decided to research the history of his family. He wasn't sure what drove the decision: whether it was the grief, or just the need to be doing something, however little. In the attic at the top of the house, he had found a few boxes of old photograph albums and newspaper clippings that his predecessors had left behind. There were journals and books, notepads and old diaries. The type that the main character in a horror film would blow the dust off to discover some long-forgotten secret. In addition to this, he had begun researching online and printing off every reference he could find to Perkins Farm and Cobweb Cottage. And now, all this information was in front of him. As each pile reached its optimum height, it would lose stability and flood over to the next pile.

Ian stood and stared at the paperwork. In its current state, it was impossible to tell whether anything was out of place. He sighed, and committed himself to sorting it.

Under the huge window to his right was his desk. It was positioned so he could take in the full view down to the bottom of the drive and across the front garden. Again, nothing seemed out of place. The chair was where he had left it the day before, pushed firmly underneath so its arms weren't showing. The silver metal bin, in the same place. The top of the chair obscured the surface of the desk, so he slowly took a pace forwards. Aside from the computer and printer, which stood alongside one another, and the silver lamp, the desk was empty. Just as he had left it.

The shelves on the wall above the computer were untouched.

The rows of miniature action figures and the mugs filled with pens and pencils were as they had been the night before. The hands of the clock showed the right time.

At first, he had put the strange occurrences down to simple absentmindedness. The first time, he remembered, he had entered his study and found one of the piles of paperwork removed from the piano and piled instead on the floor to the left of his desk. He couldn't recall moving the papers, but also couldn't say for sure that he hadn't. That particular morning, he had asked Rachel whether she was the one who had moved the papers. He'd been greeted with silence and a face that burned with contempt.

The look still wrangled Ian.

It was unlikely there was any coming back from that. Unless, well, unless his research uncovered the truth.

Another morning, Ian had entered the room to find the computer monitor face down on the desk, its screen resting on top of the keyboard. He had stared at it for some time, wondering whether it could have somehow fallen. He concluded that wasn't possible.

Another day, pens and pencils had been taken from the shelves and lined up in a neat, straight line across the middle of the desk. Most recently, the walnut surface had been barely visible beneath the Post-it notes that had been individually removed and carefully wallpapered across the desk.

After each strange occurrence he'd chosen not to ask Rachel if she'd been involved. He didn't want to see that look again.

Ian had no recollection of whether he was actually responsible. He didn't trust his memory anymore. In fact, he didn't trust his mind at all. It had been required to cope with a little too much just recently. Right now, if he'd been asked whether he was male or not, he would have had to go to the bathroom to make absolutely sure. Added to this, his mind was filled to capacity with all his research. He was sure he could feel his brain swelling as he took in more and more information, pushing the inside of his skull like the contents of an overfilled bag of refuse.

Today, though, was not one of those days. Everything was as Ian had left it the night before. Over the week, he had taken to entering the study just before bed and taking a number of photographs on his phone. That way he had a definitive record of how he'd left the room. Now, he could try to narrow down the window of time in which these unusual events were occurring. Since he had begun his nocturnal checks, no further incidents had arisen.

Ian generally spent the afternoon in the study prior to Harry returning. He was fortunate to be able to work from home in his role as editor of a film website. The website collected reviews, comments and news from the film industry worldwide and Ian was responsible for its content. He was also required to write his own daily blog on the site. Initially, this had been time-consuming, and he would spend six or seven hours a day carefully structuring his sentences, honing his comment. Latterly, the blog took less than an hour to write. He had lost interest; there simply wasn't room in his mind. His employers remained happy, though: the website was popular and received enough interest from advertisers to return the owners a nice profit after paying Ian and the other contributors. Ian suspected that they didn't even bother to read his columns anymore. As long as the money came in each month, they were satisfied. And it suited Ian as well. He was happy, because the job was easy and it paid the bills. But more importantly, it left him plenty of time for the two things that brought him any joy: Harry and his research.

He would spend most of the afternoon in the study, until the moment he heard the excited footsteps in the hall outside and the tiny knock on the thick wooden door. At that moment he would close down his machine and open the door to let Harry in.

He swiped his finger underneath the large monitor and the screen burst into life. As the machine rumbled through its start-up procedure, he stared out of the large window, down the long drive. The window was actually eighteen small panes of glass separated by wood that had once been painted white. The paint was now missing in most places and what remained had separated and curled over like a surfer's wave. Condensation attacked each of the individual panes, making it only possible to see through the top half. In the winter, ice would actually gather on the inside. Replacing the window was on Ian's list. But many things were on Ian's list and rarely did anything get crossed out.

He spotted a fox at the end of the drive, its ginger coat soaked by the last cloudburst. It turned its head toward the house. Ian stood and wiped his sleeve across a couple of the panes to get a better look. It was a big fox, definitely male. It was too far away to make out its features, but Ian was sure it could see him.

The fox took a step forward and sniffed the ground. Ian used his sleeve again on the window. The fox looked directly at him. Then something startled it. Ian couldn't see what it was. The fox was looking back down the track it had just come from. Then it turned and hurried down the lane. Ian watched until it disappeared behind the giant sycamore tree. It never reappeared on the other side. The weight of the rain on the branches of the tree made it look more threatening than usual. Through the wet branches, high up in the tree, Ian could just see the red roof and red door of the treehouse he had built for Harry the previous summer.

The computer made a sudden ping, signifying that it was finally awake and Ian had new emails to deal with. It was a welcome distraction. Ian sat down in his chair, happy to leave the dark, unforgiving heaviness of the tree behind the steamed-up glass.

SIX

Once Uncle Stephen was inside the house and safely out of sight, the two boys simultaneously began laughing. Ian wasn't quite sure why. It may have been relief. Whatever the reason, it was contagious and his chest pumped in and out in unison with his shoulders. Stuart's did the same.

The laughter continued for several minutes; each time it seemed like it was about to end, Ian would look at Stuart and they would begin again. Around the time Ian felt that his insides might tear from the aching, the laughter subsided, like the fade towards the end of a song. Deep breaths and staccato giggles pricked the summer sky. Ian pushed his head into Stuart's shoulder and Stuart rubbed his brother's hair playfully.

They shared the remainder of the water, both keen to ensure that each received the same amount. After all, they had to be certain that they could both make it back across the lava to the house when the time came. The look on their father's face as he had followed Uncle Stephen inside suggested that they shouldn't enter the house until he gave the signal it was okay. The boys laid their heads awkwardly against the foot of the tree, their legs outstretched, shaded beneath the strange branch that pointed toward the house. It was quiet.

Ian lifted his head slightly. "Stuart?" he said. It was one of those things children say when they

don't know what they're going to say next. A name –
ssssstttttttrrrrrrrreeeeeeeeeeetttttcccccccched out – with a
hopeful inflection to gauge whether they have the attention of
the person they're speaking to. Ian would consider what to say
next once he had a response.

Stuart didn't answer; he was looking at the cottage,
seemingly in a dream. Ian was happy with the silence and
rested his head back against the tree. He buried his fingers
into the ground, excavating the soil around the roots that were
protruding through the ground, and stared at the cottage.

It was an unusual place really. When it was originally
built, it would have looked like the type of property a child
draws when given a crayon and asked to picture a house. An
unimaginative white-washed rectangle. A red roof meeting at
its highest point in the centre. Six large windows ran along the
upper floor, and beneath them were four identical windows. In
the centre, a large, almost oversized front door was flanked by
two stone columns that reached up to the roof. The columns
seemed out of place, as if they had only been added because the
previous occupants could afford to do so. They added nothing
to the cottage; simply a pointless statement of grandeur and
affluence. There were two black metal crosses on either side
of the columns. A matching pair was visible at the back of the
house. Huge steel rods connected the crosses together, keeping
the walls parallel. Above the door, it was still possible to make
out the crumbling digits – 1808 – carved into a giant sandstone
lintel.

41

Since the original build, generation after generation of the Perkins family had arrived and departed, each adding their own personal touches to the property. The original structure remained and, seemingly without thought to the overall aesthetic, the occupants added whatever they needed. It was entirely practical. If there was a lack of storage space, they would simply build an area for storage onto the cottage. If they needed a downstairs bathroom, they would attach one. And, to save costs, they used whatever materials they could find on the farm.

To the left of the house, from where the boys were lying, was a huge, red-brick lean-to. It came down from roof to floor, and stuck out like a giant chimney flume. In it were three windows, smaller and at different levels to those in the rest of the house. The whole property leaned toward the extension and it looked as if it had been hurriedly put up to stop the house collapsing to the ground. Just behind the extension, it was possible to make out the slate roof of the huge barn that ran alongside the back garden.

On the right of the property, where the drive met the house, a further single-storey extension had been added perhaps thirty or forty years earlier. It consisted of one large window and an ugly expanse of pebble-dashed wall topped by a flat roof. Ian's father had tried to cover the wall with creeping plants. None had survived.

However unusual and uninviting the cottage looked, it was a great place for the boys to grow up. Fields surrounded the property on all sides. Small woodland areas peppered the landscape. The boys could easily find terrain to transform into the desert of the Alamo for their toy cowboys, and places where their plastic marines could attempt to conquer the wet swampland of the jungles of Vietnam. There were streams to cool off in during the hot, humid summer months, and ponds and small lakes to slide across in the winter. These were the places where adventures from the furthest outskirts of their imaginations were formed.

In many ways, the property reflected the history of the family. The haphazard nature of the structure and the paper-over-the-cracks mentality were, without question, Perkins family traits. The building, not unlike the relationships between the family members, was prone to collapse at any time.

The silence of the afternoon was broken less than ten minutes after Uncle Stephen entered the house. He was leaving. Now. Right this minute.

Ian stretched, his daydream interrupted by the noise. He nudged Stuart. Stuart groaned lightly.

Uncle Stephen backed out of the front door. He had his arms raised and was shaking his head. Ian began tapping Stuart repeatedly on the thigh. Stuart opened his eyes, and Ian pointed toward the door. Stuart looked over, then sat upright immediately. Moments later, their father walked out of the front door. He was holding a shotgun. One hand was on the barrel, the other poised near the trigger.

Uncle Stephen continued backing away, his eyes transfixed by the gun. He was shaking his head again and again. He stumbled momentarily over the small flowerbed that separated the lawn from the gravel drive.

As Ian watched, his mother rushed out of the front door and pulled at his father's shoulder. Dad stopped for a moment and turned, wriggling free from Mum's hand as he did so. Ian couldn't see Dad's face, but he could tell from the look on Mum's face that she should keep her distance. Her arm dropped and she stood with both hands over her mouth, staring as Dad took another step forward.

Uncle Stephen had continued to move backwards. He was almost past the large wheel of the tractor, his hands feeling the rubber behind him to keep his balance.

He was adjacent to the tree now, no more than thirty feet from the boys. Ian moved closer to his brother. The sudden movement caught Dad's eye, and he realised for the first time that the boys were outside.

"Move!" he shouted.

Both boys jumped.

Uncle Stephen scrambled back towards his car.

"House. Now!"

The two boys rushed to their feet, tearing their bare knees on the roots of the tree beneath them. They ran breathlessly down the garden.

"Come on, quickly," Dad barked, using the gun barrel to direct them toward the house. They made their way past him and stood in the doorway alongside Mum, one on each side. Their knees bled.

Dad strode forward and raised the gun to chest height as he walked. Uncle Stephen had reached the bonnet of his car, and he scrambled to get around to the driver's door. His brother approached. He was stuck.

"Inside. All of you!" Dad shouted.

Mum shepherded the boys into the house; they didn't dare look over their shoulders as they moved. She closed the front door and led them down the hall and through into the kitchen at the back of the house.

She pulled out a chair for each of them and instructed them to sit down. Then she opened the cupboard under the sink and removed a large roll of cotton wool, the type you see in a hospital. She ripped a piece from the roll and ran the tap until the water warmed. The boys watched in silence. Neither could feel the blood that trickled slowly toward their socks.

Mum approached, and kneeled in front of Ian. She looked up from the floor. Her eyes were red, her cheeks blotchy.

"Right," she said, trying to bring strength to her cracking voice, "I need you to be really brave. This will sting."

Ian nodded.

And then outside there was a bright flash.

As the wet cotton wool made contact with Ian's skin, every head turned simultaneously toward the front door.

To the place that the gunshot had come from.

SEVEN

The horizon sucked in the last stripe of pink, leaving the rest of the sky a steel grey. Ian stretched backwards in his chair, threading his fingers into one another before cracking them above his head.

There were only three emails in his inbox, and only two new film releases of any interest this week. At this time of year the industry was usually quiet. Of course, a smattering of indie art-house releases came out each week. Now, these were the real films – the ones that had been made on a minute budget in Romania or some other Eastern European country. Films that dealt with real problems, unaffected by the Hollywood gloss that most cinema-goers have to stomach. Initially, Ian had covered these films in his daily updates, but soon his employers asked him to remove such content. Apparently, it was losing them visitors to the site. Instead, he was to focus on whichever celebrity had stumbled over drunk on a night out, or been spotted wearing pyjamas in her own garden. This was the content that the readers wanted, he was told. After a brief debate, he was left with no alternative but to follow their instruction.

And so, Hollywood won, as it always did. And the smaller releases were seen only by a handful of committed film buffs, just as Hollywood dictated. Ian read through each of the reviews submitted to him by his other contributors, correcting small parts of each before posting them live on the site. He then went into the archived content and resurrected a few 'top ten' lists for his audience. People loved that. It was lazy content at best, but Ian didn't care: he was getting paid for it. 'Top Ten Mafia Movies' and 'Top Ten Films Starring Drew Barrymore' were up in minutes, and he promptly logged out of the site.

Ian left the study to make a drink. As he pulled the door open, Rachel was passing. She swerved slightly to avoid the door opening onto her. It wasn't the first time this had happened over the course of the last few weeks. He was beginning to think that Rachel had taken to standing behind the door, listening, trying to work out what was happening inside.

The irony was that if she wanted to know, she simply had to ask. Unfortunately, they were near past the point of talking now.

Ian apologised as Rachel brushed past him. She didn't avert her stare from straight down the hall. She didn't say a word. Ian saw her hand on the post at the bottom of the stairs, and then it was gone. He listened to the sound of her feet as she slowly made her way up the stairs. Each step was evidently a huge effort. He heard the click of her bedroom door closing behind her, and made his way into the kitchen.

He distinctly remembered the pact they had made. It was a vivid memory that he had stored to the tiniest detail. It had appeared and flown around his mind every single day since the incident. It was important that he could remember. If he

47

could do that; he could work forwards to try to understand why he and Rachel were now in the position they were in. He had brought it to mind and retraced every single aspect of that evening. He was confident that if he was questioned, he would bet his life – no, Harry's life – on his getting every single word of the conversation absolutely correct. As he waited for the kettle to boil, he challenged himself to take his own test.

The corner of the pub was dark. A single wall light shone down on Ian, Rachel and a watercolour of a red tractor ploughing yellow fields. The picture was an original, displayed in a gaudy gold frame. It was by an artist called Jenkinson and a little cardboard price tag hung from it. Yours for just fifteen pounds. The pub was busy; an excitable chatter bounced off the stone floors and part-exposed stone walls. They had just finished eating. Rachel had fish and chips, without vinegar of course. Ian had the same. He smiled at Rachel and wiped his mouth with a napkin. He threw it down on top of his plate, to signify that he had finished. Half a pint of bitter remained in Ian's glass. Rachel was drinking orange juice. Fizzy. It was their one-year anniversary; the meal was a way of celebrating.

A couple sat at the table next to them. The man had spilled egg down his shirt and his wife jokingly commented that he wasn't fit to go out anywhere. She had dark brown hair, neatly set, and wore a jade-green necklace made of heavy beads. Her ring matched. The man wore a multi-coloured checked shirt: white, red and yellow. If the woman hadn't pointed out the egg, you would never have seen it; it would have remained lost in the pattern. Throughout the meal they had joined in Ian and Rachel's conversation once or twice. They told them that they had been together for twenty-six years that day. The man made the usual joke about doing less time for murder, and the four of them laughed.

The waitress took orders for coffee and dessert. Ian ordered the treacle sponge pudding and another half of beer. Rachel ordered cheesecake and a coffee. The couple at the table alongside decided not to have dessert. The woman had received a text message, and all of a sudden they seemed in a rush. They said their farewells and left.

Ian sensed the conversation was about to turn to more serious issues. He could tell from the look on Rachel's face as her eyes followed the couple out of sight. Ian pulled his chair slightly closer to Rachel. She smiled and took his hand.

"Let's not ever do that," she said.

"What?"

She nodded to the table the couple had vacated. "Talk like they did. Even for a second."

"I think they were only joking," Ian said.

"I know," said Rachel quietly. "It's just, I think we're different to them. To everyone."

"How do you mean?"

Rachel gripped Ian's hand more tightly and looked into his eyes. He could see a film of clear liquid gathering. She sniffed. He was sure she was about to cry.

"What's up?" Ian said.

She looked down and then back at him. "I *really* think we're different. I think we can conquer anything. Together."

Ian felt his hand getting sticky. He wasn't good at this sort of thing. He loved her unconditionally: simple. To him, that was it. "We can," he reassured her, "definitely."

"We just have to agree one thing," she said.

"What?" he said as gently as he could, in an attempt to avert her tears.

"We have to agree that whatever happens, we will always talk."

"We will."

She squeezed his hand harder. He felt the bones fighting for space. With her spare hand she cupped his chin, and she looked directly into his eyes. It was as if she was trying to read his mind.

"I mean it," she said. "Whatever happens, we will always be honest and always talk."

Ian knew she'd been hurt before. It was an easy pact to make. This was, after all, his definition of love. Speak your mind. Say what you feel. It wasn't going to be difficult.

"I agree."

"Pact?" she said.

"Pact," he agreed.

Their hands separated, and moments later the waitress arrived and placed their desserts on the table in front of them.

The kettle clicked and the red light went off.

"Every single word," Ian said to himself as he spooned the coffee into the cup. And he was right. He remembered every detail and every word. Had it been possible to play a video of the night they made the pact, he would have scored full marks for his recollection. One hundred per cent correct. The fact that he and Rachel had failed to keep the pact was, without question, the most ironic thing.

Ian returned to the study and closed the door behind him. He could now get down to the thing that was driving him: his research. He would find the answer within. He would fix this problem, and he and Rachel would return to how they were before. He checked his watch: he had a couple of hours before Harry returned.

He carried a large pile of papers from the piano and spread them on the desk in front of him. In the pile was a collection of rough scribblings, written on the back of old envelopes and different notepads and pastel coloured Post-its. The majority of the papers though, consisted of print-outs from online research that he had found over the previous month. Near the bottom of the pile was a thick brown envelope. It was marked 'R. S. Perkins'. He recognised those initials from something he had printed out earlier that week. It was around here somewhere.

He flicked through the papers quickly. Nothing. He began again, this time more slowly. His eyes scanned each page, one by one. Some of the pages were one- or two-line notes in his own writing. Others were paragraph upon paragraph of text, some in minute fonts and others in fonts so large that parts of the sentences were cut off on the right-hand side of the page.

No, it wasn't in this pile, he concluded. He spun his chair toward the piano and stared at the rest of his paperwork. He narrowed his eyes, hoping to draw to mind where he had seen the name. *It could be anywhere in all this lot,* he thought.

He walked over to the piano and began flicking through the top few pages of each pile. They all looked pretty much the same – sheets and sheets of paper everywhere. Nothing was triggering his memory. There was so much information. He needed some kind of system. At this rate, he was never going to be able to draw any conclusion. And the longer it took, the less chance there was that Rachel would be waiting for him at the end.

Time had moved on. The clock above his desk told Ian that Harry would be home in less than half an hour. He sat back down at his desk and peeled open the brown envelope. It smelled strongly of rubber, of old adhesive. He reached inside and pulled out three small pocket books. Each had a hardcover and was bound in leather. Two blue. One red. He opened the red one.

Inside the front of the book, in faded blue ink, was beautiful cursive script writing. In the top corner was written 'Robert Perkins'. Beneath the name, in the same handwriting, was a date – 1936. Ian turned the yellowed page, which cracked as it separated from the next page for the first time in perhaps fifty years. Printed in dark ink in the centre was the word

'Diary'. On the opposite side was a grid showing the days for each month of the year. Ian flicked to where the diary began. It was set out showing a week over two pages. There was little space to make notes, which Ian quickly realised was probably the reason Robert Perkins had selected such a small book.

It read:

1st January (New Year's Day) Mary arrived.
Had lamb and potatoes. Overcast.

Ian collected a Post-it from the side and scribbled 'Mary?' on it. He read further:

2nd January   Work. Rain.
3rd January   Work. Rain.
4th January   Saturday. Peaceful. Cloudy.

The diary continued in the same way until the end of January. Ian was disappointed that he had collected only one further name to work on. And that was on the first day he had turned to: New Year's Day. He was also disappointed that the potential treasure trove of information had turned into a laconic weather summary. It seemed that 'Robert Perkins' was a man of few words. Or not particularly observant.

As he flicked the page over to February, he heard a light banging on the study door. He placed the diary on the desk and opened the door.

He was greeted by a huge smile. It was surrounded by a thin layer of hardened chocolate.

"Daddy!"

Harry was proudly holding out a large piece of paper. Ian reached down and scooped Harry up into his arms. As he carried him over to the desk, he kissed his forehead repeatedly.

"Come and sit down with me," Ian said. "What have you got there?"

Ian sat in the chair and lifted Harry onto his knee. Harry held up the picture. Ian noticed that the thick blue and green paint that covered it was already beginning to crack. Curls of pasta were randomly glued across it.

"Wow!" said Ian. It was the type of 'wow lie' that comes naturally to parents of infant children. The intonation in his voice was enough to stretch Harry's smile even wider.

"Can you see what it is, Daddy?"

"Of course I can."

"What is it then?"

"Er, is it a snail on the grass?"

Harry threw his head back and laughed. "Nooooo, Daddy!"

Ian smiled.

"It's not a snail. It's a boat, silly!"

Ian took the picture from Harry and pretended to study it.

"Oh yeah," he said. "Of course it is."

Harry kept giggling, as if he had heard the funniest joke ever. Ian licked two of his fingers and rubbed the remains of whatever Harry had been eating from around his mouth. Harry wriggled to escape. When Ian had finished, Harry turned to the desk and placed both his hands on the papers. He turned to Ian.

"What's all this mess, Daddy?"

Ian laughed. "It's Daddy's work, Harry."

"It's messy work, Daddy."

"I know. But it's important work."

"Why?"

"Because I'm finding out about our family."

"Why?"

"Well, because when Daddy was younge–"

"What's that, Daddy?" Harry was pointing to a small metal cowboy figure on the shelf above the desk.

"It's a cowboy."

"A toy?"

"Not for playing with, though."

"Aw." Harry's face dropped. "Why?"

"It was Uncle Stuart's toy."

"Uncle Stuart who lives with the angels in heaven?"

"Yes, that's right."

"Oh," said Harry. "I'm hungry."

"Right then," said Ian, lifting Harry to his chest and pushing himself out of his chair. "Let's get something to eat."

EIGHT

The rest of that evening was quiet – aside from the echo of the gunshot, which seemed to permanently ring in Ian's ears. He and Stuart shared a quiet meal with Mum. Their father's absence at the dining room table went unmentioned. After they had finished dinner, they were sent up to bed early, their knees decorated with coral-coloured fabric plasters.

The bedroom that they shared was at the front of the house. It was uncomfortably hot, having drunk in the blistering sun for the entirety of the day, and dark: the curtains were already firmly closed, in a vain attempt to cool the air. Thin rectangles of daylight sneaked in around the edges to reveal the room, compact and small. In it were two beds, one under the window, the other parallel against the wall, separated by an oversized pine bedside table with a small red lamp. All four walls were covered in the same wallpaper; a repeating pattern of superheroes. When Ian had first been shown the room he hadn't been able to believe it. Adorning the walls with Superman and Batman wasn't the type of thing that his parents, his father especially, would have allowed. A waste of money. He imagined his father's gruff voice. 'What's wrong with painting the walls white?'

Ian climbed into his bed, next to the window. He was tired. He watched as Mum embraced Stuart, his brother's neck

56

arching awkwardly as he lifted himself from bed. She whispered something to him as she stood straight; Ian couldn't make out what she said. Stuart flopped back down and Mum tucked him in, kissing his forehead. Then, as she did every night, she walked the gap between their beds, tucking their sheets firmly under the mattress. Ian complained about the heat and she reached across his bed and opened a small window. Then she pulled the curtains across again, accidentally leaving a small gap.

Half in and half out of the room, she wished them goodnight. She warned them not to talk or she would "be back". She left with a frown, after telling them to "get some good sleep".

As the latch on the door clicked shut, Stuart kicked off his duvet and turned to Ian.

"Can you see?" he whispered.

Ian glared. Stuart knew the rules. They weren't allowed to talk.

"I said, can you see?" Stuart repeated.

Ian shook his head rapidly and planted his head deep in the pillow. He wished that Stuart would just go to sleep. He didn't want his mother to "be back", whatever that meant. Worse still would be the sound of his father's feet on the stairs. He felt a finger on his shoulder and slowly turned his head. Stuart was stretched across the gap, a human bridge between the beds.

"Oi!" Stuart demanded in a whisper. "Can you see? Out there?"

Ian put his index finger over his lips, shushing his brother.

57

The floor of the landing outside the bedroom door creaked. Ian felt his heart stop, just for a second. Stuart froze rigid across the gap. Ian closed his eyes tightly and struggled to pull the duvet over his face. He just wished he was asleep. He could hear a sound but couldn't make out what it was over his rapid breathing. At any moment, he expected the bedroom door to fly open and his mother to claw back the covers from his face.

He listened harder and realised that the sound was closer. He felt the side of his mattress lower, turning him ever so slightly to his left. His ears felt fuzzy, as if he couldn't hear properly – that wishy-washy feeling that happened sometimes after swimming in the lake. His heart stopped again. He felt a presence right next to him and took a deep breath, encouraging himself to see what was there. He counted backwards from three in his head and pulled back the cover. There was Stuart, kneeling on his bed, his finger reaching across the bed for the curtain.

Stuart frowned at him, his eyes threatening Ian not to speak. Ian closed his eyes again and lay as still as he could. A moment later, he felt the weight release and heard Stuart softly scramble back to the safety of his own bed. Ian opened his eyes and looked blankly through the half-light to his brother.

"His car's gone," Stuart whispered.

Ian mouthed, *What?*

"Uncle Stephen's car. It's gone."

Both boys must have heard the creak of the landing floorboard at the same time, because less than a second later they were hiding their faces underneath their duvets, their mouths open, their eyes shut.

Exactly how they imagined they looked when they slept.

The following morning was unusual for two reasons.

The first reason was that when Ian finally came downstairs for breakfast, his mother, father and brother were already in the kitchen. He expected to see Mum and Stuart. But Dad? This happened rarely, if ever. Perhaps at Christmas-time, just maybe. His father was usually miles away, out in the fields somewhere by the time anybody awoke.

The second reason was that the table had apparently been set for a banquet. Racks of freshly made toast lay in the middle, along with bowls of apples and pears from the orchard that had been peeled and chopped into small pieces. Marmalade and two types of jam lay alongside the antique, egg-shell-blue butter dish. The butter dish was another addition to the morning table that usually only appeared at Christmas. Perhaps Dad took it out with him on the tractor every day?

Mum stood by the huge range oven, the kettle whistling alongside her. She rubbed her hands on a dirty cotton tea towel and offered a hollow smile. Ian smiled back. Something was wrong. He looked over to Stuart, and saw he was sitting upright, rigid in his chair.

Dad beckoned Ian over to the table. He had a cream bandage wrapped around his hand. A large safety pin held it tightly together near his wrist. Ian stayed where he was. He didn't like this scene at all.

"Come and sit down, Ian," said Dad, smiling. He gestured with his injured hand. It reminded Ian of a seal's flipper.

Ian smiled awkwardly. His feet wouldn't allow him to move closer. It somehow seemed like a movement into impending danger.

"What's the matter, son?" said Dad.

Son? He never calls me 'son', thought Ian. He turned to Mum, looking for comfort. She smiled again.

"Go on," she said. "The toast is getting cold."

Ian stayed where he was.

"Ian, come and sit down," repeated Dad. His tone was getting more impatient.

Mum came over and put a gentle arm around Ian and guided him slowly toward the table. She pulled out his chair and tapped the seat with her fingers.

Ian shuffled slowly onto the seat and stared at the cutlery.

"Tea?" Mum called from behind him.

"Good idea," said Dad. "Make a pot."

Ian looked up through his fringe and glimpsed his father. Dad looked like he had been crying.

Ian's mother poured the tea and flattened her skirt behind her, before sitting on the chair next to him. He pulled a piece of thick white toast from the rack and placed it on his plate. Mum pushed the butter dish across the white tablecloth. Ian picked up his knife and cut into the corner of the butter, before depositing a small lemon-coloured pyramid onto his toast. After a few seconds of Ian struggling to crush the hard yellow lump into a spreadable substance, Mum took the knife from him and buttered the toast. He bit into it. It was cold.

Nobody spoke.

The slurp of a drink or crunch of a bite echoed around the silence of the room. Something was very wrong. Ian was finding it difficult to chew; the noise sounded so loud. It was even harder to swallow, the dry toast lodging at the back of his tongue. On more than one occasion he had to wash it down with a gulp of tea. It tasted foul.

Ian looked across to Stuart again, hoping for a helpful glance or to instigate a conversation. Perhaps Stuart would be brave enough to say something. He was the eldest, after all. Stuart looked away.

Ian glanced at Dad. He was now staring directly at the centre of the table, thick furrows of skin separating his eyebrows. They reminded Ian of the toast standing in the rack, or the ploughed fields that he could see in the background behind where his father was sitting.

Mum sighed gently and sipped from her tea. Ian looked at her, and she smiled solemnly. She reached over to her husband's bandaged hand and stroked his fingers. He looked at her and then into the space that separated Ian from Stuart.

Dad cleared his throat.

And sighed.

And took another drink of tea.

Ian noticed Mum was still stroking Dad's fingers, but more rapidly than before, as if coaxing him to shatter the atmosphere with words. Dad looked over at his wife. Their stare seemed to last forever. Ian's eyes stung; he felt like he was going cry.

Then, at last, his father spoke.

"Okay," he said. "Boys. I have some bad news."

Ian felt a lump in his throat. He looked at Stuart; he was gazing upwards directly into Dad's face, listening intently – he looked like a baby bird about to be fed. Dad reached out and rubbed Stuart's cheek with his good hand. He then placed it on his own face, resting his chin on the palm.

"Go on," Mum said quietly.

Through his fingers, Dad delivered the news that Uncle Stephen was dead. He managed to keep himself from crying as he told them of the phone call he had received, just before he was about to leave for work.

Earlier that morning, a local man had been walking his dog a few miles from their home. The man let his dog off the lead, and the dog led him to a small, thin track that separated two fields. It was a track that Ian and his father had travelled on many times – raised up from the fields, with deep tractor tracks moulded into the hardened mud. The dog raced ahead. The man travelled up one side of the dusty track, and as he reached the top he saw a vehicle a few hundred feet ahead in the distance. The vehicle was upside down.

The man rushed down to the vehicle to investigate. When he reached the front, he saw the body, half in the car, half in the field. It was clear that the man was dead. Uncle Stephen had a large puncture in the side of his neck, the blood crisp and dry around the wound.

The man turned and walked several miles back over the fields to the outskirts of the village where he lived. There, he reported the accident. The police telephoned Ian's father at just after seven that morning to let him know the news. They would collect a statement later that day.

Ian felt the lump in his throat subside. He knew that he was supposed to cry but he didn't feel anything. He looked again at Stuart; his brother looked puzzled. Mum squeezed her husband's fingers. Dad slurped his tea again, his throat dry from the story he had told.

"The funeral will be next week," Mum calmly told the boys. Ian nodded. Stuart just stared.

"We'll all be attending," said Dad. "It's only right."

Ian stared at his half-eaten toast. He wasn't hungry.

"If you've finished, you can get down now," said Mum.

Stuart pushed himself up from the table and walked quickly from the room. He seemed glad to escape. Ian followed more slowly, taking another glimpse of Dad as he left. He looked different from the day before. His face was paler. Older.

When Ian reached the door leading to the hall, he crouched behind the door frame and peeked in. He saw Dad return Mum's smile.

"You did well," Mum said across the table.

Ian could see one side of Dad's face. His eyes were on the

chair where Ian had been sitting.

Dad grunted. He didn't seem pleased.

"You did. It's not an easy thing to talk about," Mum implored a little more loudly.

Dad shook his head, then rested his face in his hand.

"Are you worried the boys will find out?"

"I just don't want them living in the shadow of it."

"Well, they needn't know about the curse."

"Let's try to keep it that way." Dad turned to her. "At least until they're old enough to understand."

"Do you believe in it?"

"I don't know. I didn't..." He paused, shaking his head. "I just don't know."

Ian saw his father stand and he did the same, as quietly as he could, before gingerly racing up the stairs.

NINE

Saturday was the best and the worst day of the week.

It was the best because the house was empty all day.

It was the worst because the house was empty all day.

By the time Ian awoke – whatever time that was – Rachel had already gone. Sometimes in the dead of the night, when the nightmares came and clawed at Ian until he awoke, he would get up and wander the cottage just to escape the ghostly figures that he imagined surrounding his bed. It would usually be in that horrible time period when it is still dark outside and the entire world seems contently asleep. When that happened, he would take himself into the kitchen, turn on all the lights and wait for the dawn to break. Sometimes he would wake and find his head pushed firmly into the kitchen table. If it was a Saturday, he could guarantee that regardless of what time and in which room he woke, Rachel would have already gone. Ian had begun to wonder whether on Friday night, Rachel waited for him to go to bed, and then quickly dressed, sneaked downstairs and left in the dead of the night.

Rachel's mother only had one grandchild: Harry. From almost the time he was born, Ian and Rachel had taken him over to see his 'Nana' every Saturday afternoon. In the early days, they lived much closer to her. Since they had moved to Cobweb Cottage, a visit to Rachel's mother necessitated an overnight stay. Rachel had decided, quite correctly, that a three-hour drive each way was probably a little too much for Harry to endure in one day.

In the last three or four months, Ian had been gently excluded from the visits. In many ways that suited him. The visits were always cordial enough, but usually as the day dragged on the conversation would drift to updates on old family friends and other people Ian didn't know. He would nod and smile at the right times, while thinking of a million other things he could be doing. In the early evening, he would bath Harry, give him his supper and tuck him up in bed. After that, the rest of the evening consisted of trips back and forth to the kitchen, collecting and serving various drinks and nibbles to the ladies whilst they chatted.

Maybe things were that way because Rachel's parents were divorced and twenty years earlier her mother had vowed never to have another man. It was a promise she had kept, and since that day her attention had been wholly focused on Rachel – and latterly, on Harry.

For all of the relief that Ian's recent exclusion from the weekly visits brought, it meant, however, a full day and night without Harry. In fact, it was more than that. The visits had begun to stretch out that little bit longer, and now Ian was unlikely to see his wife and son until late on Sunday afternoon. And with the current state of their marriage, time with Harry was the only thing that kept Ian going.

Ian entered the kitchen and planted himself down at the

range table, in his usual place. Rachel's absence meant that he could play music without a tut or sneer. *August and Everything After*. An all-time favourite. Leaves danced and skipped around the garden, and Ian watched them surge as the wind caught them before they drifted for a while and fell to the lawn. They were almost alive, darting in unison like a huge flock of birds. The back of the house was similar to the front. In all directions, as far as the eye could see, there were fields of yellow and green. A small dry-stone wall ran around the perimeter of the large garden. To his left, in the corner, was a stile that led out over the wall to a thousand childhood adventures. In the distance, the green leaves on the branches of the woodland trees waved from side to side. They reminded Ian of arms aloft at a rock festival. He made a mental note to attend a concert again soon. It had been years. Too long.

The album finished and Ian pressed play again. If the music hadn't finished and Ian hadn't suddenly become aware of the silence, then it is doubtful that he would have even known that time had passed. So many days were like this now. Just drifting. Waiting for something to happen. There were times when he felt inspired to grasp the day by the scruff of the neck and shake himself into action. He was aware that life was short, precious. But somehow he couldn't do anything about it.

Days drifted by, days staring through the window.

Watching the sun move from right to left.

Time and time again.

Over and over and over again.

The only time that mattered was time with Harry. He had tried and tried with Rachel, to the extent that he was now fatigued from the fight. He couldn't remember any arguments as such, just a curtain of disappointed silence. Single-word answers. Tuts. Or, worse still, not even an acknowledgement of his existence. God, he had tried. Whatever comment or question or suggestion he had made ultimately led to the same place: spoken or inferred rejection.

Still, for a long time he'd repeatedly bounced back like an excitable puppy. He had read books to help repair their marriage, to lift them from the situation and get them back to where they'd once been. He would read late into the night, eagerly sucking in and storing the words of advice. Invariably, he would seize the opportunity in the kitchen the following morning to pass on the guidance he had read the night before. He hoped that something would trigger in Rachel's mind and she would realise that it was time for them to move on; that there would be an awakening inside her, and whatever was holding her down would suddenly loosen its grip and she would begin to see clearly again. He worked on the basis that the more he read and imparted, the more chance there was that something would resonate. So far, it hadn't.

But he wasn't about to stop trying. He was passing on advice from people who had *actually* been in their situation, sensible words suggesting helpful things that they should do as a couple to draw closer together. But herein lay the problem. All the books offered exercises that they should do as a couple. And unfortunately for Ian, only one half of the couple was trying.

His brain physically hurt from the thinking he had done. It felt like a constant pressure inside his head, giant hands squeezing his brain tightly, crushing it. He had been through the comfort-and-care stage with Rachel, and the what-can-I-do-to-make-things-better? stage. Both had been met with the same silence. He had been through the angry, I've-had-enough-now-just-pull-yourself-together-and-let's-deal-with-this stage. It hadn't helped.

Now he was drained of energy. He had bounced back too many times. He was tired and out of ideas. His only hope was that once he had finally got to the truth, things would be different. Ian had to admit that this was a tiny and distant hope, like trying to find a grain of salt on a beach, but still he hoped. That one morning they'd leave their bedrooms at the same moment and meet on the landing. That they'd embrace – holding each other for what seemed like an eternity – and then part, and at that moment, just by looking into her eyes, he'd know that he'd succeeded. That they could now move on, together. It was a long shot, but the hope was really all he had left.

Bang.

Ian jumped backwards in his chair. It took him a moment to work out what had just happened. A maroon smear on the glass in front of him quickly confirmed that a bird had flown straight into the window.

The room was silent, the music long finished. Ian walked

around the edge of the table and looked down to the stone paving outside. The bird lay on its back, its neck broken. One wing twitched slightly. Ian kneeled alongside it, separated only by the glass. It was small. Its beautiful brown and black speckled feathers gleamed in the sunshine, almost as if they had been polished especially for this final flight. The feathers around its neck, however, were ruffled and twisted. A patch was missing altogether, those feathers dancing with the leaves. There Ian could see flesh, pinkish, with maroon oozing from it. The bird's eyes were wide open.

Ian went outside and crouched alongside it. He wanted to help, but he knew that there was nothing he could do. He watched silently until its wing stopped twitching and the feathers stopped their rise and fall. As the bird lay on the warm stone, it must have had an idea that its life was virtually at an end. That there was nothing more. Ian wondered what had inspired it to continue to breathe in that condition. From the moment it hit the window, it must have known it was over, its wings splayed and broken, its neck the same. Yet its tiny heart pumped blood pointlessly around its fractured body, and it kept pushing out those breaths. What drove it to keep living?

There was always a handful of empty boxes under the sink in the utility room. Rachel kept them there, for the days when Harry came home and informed them that Mrs Victory had told him he needed to bring a box to nursery to build a castle or a rocket or something similar. Ian found an old Clarks shoebox from the pair they had bought for Harry most recently, the ones he called his 'big boy shoes'.

Ian carefully scooped the little bird up and placed it in the box. It was still warm. He pushed kitchen roll around each side of it, to make it comfortable. Then, using his index and middle fingers, he gently stroked the feathers, flattening them until they lay straight again. He covered the bird with one final piece of kitchen roll and closed the lid of the box. He placed it on the kitchen table. It needed a proper burial, a moment of final dignity. He would bury it properly once he was dressed.

He pressed play and began the same album for the third time that morning.

TEN

It was the day of Uncle Stephen's funeral. Ian was uncomfortable as soon as they got in the car. His legs itched where the fabric of his new black suit rubbed against them. The material was coarse; later he would describe it as almost 'sandpapery' in texture. He was also too hot. Mum and Dad had made him wear this stupid black tie and a shirt on a day like today. The sun filled the car, making the plastic seats hot to touch and the temperature near unbearable.

Ian was sitting in the back of the car behind his mother. During the hour-long journey, he continually watched his father. The skin on Dad's face looked thick and tough, like cheap meat, the product of a life spent outside in the harshness of numerous northern winters. He remained impassive, his face plain and emotionless, his eyes never leaving the road. Once or twice, Dad took a small cloth from the side of the door and leaned out of the window, to wipe the dots of blood that used to be flies from the windscreen. He grimaced as he rubbed the liquid carcasses away. As soon as he was finished and comfortably back in his seat, his expression reverted to the same blank, unfaltering stare. Not once did he wipe away the sweat that ran like candle wax down his temples and neck.

They travelled in silence. On Ian's right, Stuart rested his head on the window and slept. From time to time the silence was broken by the sound of his head impacting with the glass as the car bumped and jarred in unison with the pot-holed roads. Not once did he wake. Mum clutched her handbag tightly throughout the journey, turning the pads of her fingers to white. Not once did she speak.

As the constant parallels of hedgerow subsided and houses began to appear, Dad's expression started to change. His left eye began to twitch slightly, an indication that something was happening inside his head; Ian wasn't sure what. Now they were surrounded by rows of small stone cottages. They passed a local greengrocer's, the pavement outside a rainbow of fruits and vegetables. Next, a coal merchant's. Two men lifted large sacks onto the back of a cart. An old dust-coloured horse waited patiently. And then more houses, lining the narrow road. Outside a small butcher's shop stood a life-size plastic butcher wearing a white coat. His eyes and enormous grin seemed to follow Ian as they approached and slowly passed. Ian turned and stared out of the window. The butcher continued to smile. As he faced the front again, Ian noticed his father grip the wheel more tightly. At the next junction they made a sharp left-hand turn and Dad pulled the car to an abrupt stop. Stuart banged his head for the last time and opened his eyes.

Ian heard the whirring of the engine slow and a click as his father removed the keys. Dad then turned his head awkwardly toward the back to address everyone in the car. Ian nudged Stuart, and he sat upright.

"We're here," said Dad grimly. "This isn't going to be a nice experience. I'll make no bones about it."

Mum nodded. Ian and Stuart looked at the floor. Ian wasn't sure why his father had intended to, and then decided against, making any bones in the first place. Come to think of it, he wasn't even sure it was possible to make bones.

"But," Dad said, rotating his finger in the direction of all three of them, "I want none of you to speak about what happened the other week at the house."

"Boys?" said Mum.

"Do you hear me?" Dad shouted.

Ian and Stuart jumped sharply, and nodded.

"Don't." Dad's pointing finger wagged in the sky, punctuating each word. "Say. Anything."

The boys nodded repeatedly. Ian felt hotter than ever. He wanted to get out.

Stuart burped and immediately apologised. Ian smirked. And then all he saw was a giant hand reaching across to him. A moment later the hand gripped his face, and he felt the insides of his cheeks touching. It hurt, and tears instantly began to gather in his eyes.

"Do you find this funny, Ian?" his father boomed.

Ian tried to shake his head, but Dad's grip made it difficult to move.

"Well, do you?" Dad shouted. He squeezed slightly more tightly and then let go, jerking Ian's head backwards.

"No more," Dad said firmly, and climbed out of the car.

The four walked along the thin pavement past numerous parked cars. Ian trailed slightly behind, kicking the loose stones as he walked. As they rounded the corner, the small terraced houses on their left became a tall grey wall. Yellow flowers grew in the cracks.

Ian picked up a stick and trailed it along the wall, following its grooves and crevices until the top began to slope and he could see what was behind. Dad turned and glared at him, and he quickly dropped the stick. The last thing Ian wanted was to get on the wrong side of Dad again. Mum seemed to sense the tension, and she took Ian's hand and led him up some wide stone steps.

At the top of the steps, a path led to the most enormous building Ian had ever seen: a church, the type he had seen on late night television on the odd occasion his parents went out together. He was sure it was the same church, the one that was momentarily illuminated by lightning before the screen returned to black. The one with the crypt; where inside Dracula was just rising from his coffin.

On either side of the giant door were two steeples that thrust into the air like giant grey rockets. People dressed in black were milling around everywhere, most looking toward the ground.

Ian had never seen so many people, and there was no clear way to the church doors. Dad led the way, craning his head one way and then the other, looking for the quickest path through, and holding the back of Stuart's neck to direct him through the crowd. Mum watched carefully, adjusting her path in unison to follow, whilst gripping Ian's hand tightly. They slowly edged forward, weaving in and out of the small groups that had gathered on the path and, in places, spilled onto the lawn where the graves began. Crumbling, moss-covered headstones were dotted on either side of the path, the etched wording now impossible to read. The plants in the soil above where the bodies lay were now nothing more than dried-out stalks.

They were near the doors now. A tall man with the remnants of white fluffy hair smiled at them. Ian noticed that he had wet eyes. He looked kind. Ian smiled back.

A small queue formed, and Ian waited alongside his mother, his face pushed into the black fabric of his father's suit. He shuffled forwards in near darkness. Then the crowd dispersed slightly and a well-dressed lady wearing a dark veil and black hat knelt down beside him. She was crying.

"Hello, Ian," she said. Then she turned. "Hello, Stuart." She pulled both boys closer to her. "Are you both okay?"

Ian smiled. He wasn't sure whether he was okay. He looked to Stuart. Stuart nodded. So Ian nodded.

The lady smiled again and pulled them into her neck. She smelled strongly of perfume. Then she stood again, and began speaking to Mum. Ian couldn't hear what was she was saying.

Ian watched as Dad spoke to an angry-looking man in a purple waistcoat. The man kept leaning into his dad's ear and speaking. Dad didn't seem to like that at all. Or the man. Dad leaned in too when he replied. Whatever he said, it didn't look very friendly to Ian. After each whisper, the two men would part and they would both get a little bit redder. Ian wondered whether they were going to fight. Dad looked far angrier than he had in the car earlier. The look on his face scared Ian.

After a few moments, Mum took Dad's arm and pulled him to the side. He didn't seem to want to move. The lady in the dark veil glared at both men, and they seemed to relax slightly. Dad nodded at the lady. He then put his arms around Ian's and Stuart's shoulders and led them through the small vestibule into the church.

Ian was directed to the very first pew at the back of the church, and he shuffled along, using the back of the seats in front for balance. Stuart followed behind him.

There was a quiet hum of noise in the church. It was the first time Ian had ever been in a church. He looked around. The ceiling was so high. It wasn't even flat either; it was arched and curved and painted in gold and white. The windows were large, all made of individual pieces of coloured glass. He followed the sunlight through each colour to where it landed. A diamond of different coloured blues danced joyfully on the wooden lectern at the front. A man stood there, wearing a tall white hat and golden robes. *That must be the vicar*, Ian thought. Everyone else looked the same. All in black. All whispering quietly.

At least it was cool in here. As they waited, Ian pulled down on the back of his trousers, trying to separate them from where the sweat had stuck them to his legs. Now and again, a stranger would turn around and smile thoughtfully at him. He would smile back. He knew that he shouldn't speak to strangers, but

77

smiling couldn't hurt. Could it?

Beside Ian, Stuart remained silent, as he had all morning. He sat with his head bowed. Ian wondered why he didn't respond to the elbow digs he kept delivering into his side.

The man at the front raised his hands and the quiet chattering stopped.

There was a crackle and then loud music began playing through the speaker above Ian. It made him jump. He had never heard the song before, but it didn't sound like the type of music they would play in a church. It was like the music that he sometimes heard on the radio in the kitchen at home. All of a sudden, the congregation all turned to the left, and Ian did the same to see what they were looking at.

Slowly and precisely, six men carried a coffin through the church. Ian recognised the man at the back. He was wearing a purple waistcoat. The men took careful steps, each in time with the next. As they passed, all Ian could see was a sad sea of faces, crying and staring across the gap toward him. He watched as the coffin arrived at the front, and the men placed it on a long table. They all took a pace backwards, away from it, and stood in a line, hanging their heads until the song finished.

The man in the white hat began to speak, and for the next half an hour everyone was made to stand and sit down several times in between singing songs from a little book. Stuart stood alongside Ian, sobbing throughout. Ian wasn't sure why he was crying, but it made him feel like doing the same. He looked at his father and saw him mouthing the words to one of the hymns; he couldn't hear any sound coming out.

Then the man in the purple waistcoat stood up. The lady with the dark veil who had greeted them when they arrived squeezed his arm before he went to the front. He talked about Uncle Stephen, about what he was like and what he liked doing. He shared some memories of things that Uncle Stephen and Uncle Stephen's mother had done together. It turned out that the lady in the dark veil was Uncle Stephen's mother. The man said that Uncle Stephen loved fast cars and that it was "fitting that he had gone that way". Ian wasn't really sure what that meant. He knew that it was sad, though, because the man in the purple waistcoat began crying as he said the words.

When the man had finished, the lady came to the front. She was crying too. She helped the man in the purple waistcoat back to his seat at the front. Then some music played again, and it was a song that Ian recognised. It was by Queen. His mother listened to it in the car. He tapped his foot as it played.

The men carried the coffin back out of the church and Ian watched his mother and father cry as it passed them. It seemed a bit strange to Ian that they would carry Uncle Stephen into the church and then back out again. *It must be what people do*, Ian thought.

After they left the church, they went to a building right next door. The building was just as busy as the church. There were people everywhere. Ian and Stuart were shown to a table where they could pick some food to eat. It was a little bit like a party, without the music. Ian filled his plate with sausage rolls and cheese and sandwiches and crisps, and followed Stuart to a row of chairs in the far corner of the room.

They sat down and ate. Between mouthfuls, Ian attempted to start a conversation with Stuart, but it was met with silence. Stuart just stared ahead with that glum look on his face. In the end, Ian gave in. He shuffled uncomfortably in his chair. He couldn't wait to get out of his suit. He hoped he'd never have to wear it again. It was so itchy. He was scratching the back of his thigh when his plate had slipped from his knees. He had only just managed to catch his food from falling to the floor. Ian laughed and nudged Stuart. Stuart didn't even flinch. He just sat staring at the floor. It was so boring.

From time to time, people would come over to Ian and say "Hello" as if they recognised him. He was polite and said "Hello" back to them. But he didn't say anything else at all, just like Dad had told him. He didn't want to risk Dad squeezing his mouth again. It was still sore from earlier. Ian knew that Stuart hadn't said anything either, because he hadn't even said "Hello" to the people. He just stayed on the same chair in the corner of the room all afternoon. And he didn't say one word.

Eventually, Dad came over to where they were sitting and told them it was time to leave. Time for home. Ian jumped up immediately; he didn't need telling twice. Stuart took Mum's hand and Ian followed them.

Just as they reached the door, the man with the purple waistcoat came over to them. His face was red, as were his eyes. He stood in the doorway, blocking their path.

"You off then?" he said angrily.

"We are," Dad said. Ian watched his face. It looked just the same as it had on the car journey that morning.

"I hope you're happy with yourself, Paul."

Ian was momentarily confused. It was unusual to hear his father's name.

"Not here, Alan," his father said.

"Not here?" the man spat. "Do you know what you've done to your mother?"

"Move."

"I won't move. Answer me."

Ian hid behind Mum's skirt, watching carefully. Alan pulled his hand back, and for a moment Ian thought he was going to throw a punch. Instead, he prodded Dad in the chest. Dad pushed the finger away. His expression changed to the same one he had when he cleared away the bodies of the flies.

Alan prodded a finger into Dad's chest again.

"Move now," Dad said through gritted teeth, pushing the finger away.

Alan took a slight step backwards. Dad moved forwards, pushing his shoulder into Alan and making him stumble slightly. He threw open the doors with both hands and they swung violently into the walls on either side. Ian was surprised that the glass didn't shatter. Dad stormed down the steps and they followed after him quickly.

As they got to the bottom, Alan shouted after them, "You

couldn't help but pass on the bloody curse, could you?"

Dad turned quickly. Ian saw his fists clench.

"Let's just go, Paul," said Mum.

"Yeah, go on, Paul. Just walk away. Like always."

Dad stood rigid. He was biting his top lip. His hands were still clenched and Ian noticed that his knuckles had turned white. He was staring directly up the steps to where Alan was standing.

"Paul. Now." Mum pulled at Dad.

Dad continued his stare. His chest was moving up and down heavily, like an over-inflated bag ready to burst at any time. For a moment, everybody stared.

And then, they were leaving.

Down the path.

Nobody looked back.

ELEVEN

As Ian stood in the shower, rubbing shampoo into his hair, he couldn't help but think that the event with the bird was some kind of sign. He wasn't sure what kind of sign yet, but he was sure it meant something. It certainly wasn't the kind of thing that happened every day. He wondered whether the bird was actually flying *to* him, bringing him some kind of message. It just hadn't considered that there had been glass separating them. And now Ian would never find out what the message was.

He stepped out of the shower and dried himself down. There was something to the idea of not being able to start a new day correctly until you'd showered away the one that had just passed. He was ready to begin today properly now. He dressed and checked his watch. It was early afternoon. There was work to be done, and he was ready. It was time to tackle this riddle once and for all.

He skipped down the stairs two at a time, turned and entered the kitchen, using the sheen of the floor and his socks to propel him. There, he grabbed his speaker and went toward the study. Then using his foot, he pushed open the door, took a step forward and placed the speaker on top of the piles of paperwork on the piano. The speaker beeped in recognition of the phone that he pulled from his pocket. He scrolled through the albums he had most recently purchased. Over the last month or two he had begun to download his music, even though it was against everything he'd previously stood for. In the past, he had got into numerous arguments about how music should only ever be listened to on vinyl. But that was before, and for now at least, it was easier this way. He scrolled through and selected Neutral Milk Hotel. He had loved this album ever since the day he purchased it. On vinyl, of course. The speaker burst into life and Ian began to sing. He spun toward the desk – and immediately stopped, his sudden burst of energy gone.

The desk was completely empty. The papers he had left scattered there the previous evening had disappeared.

He walked slowly to the chair and pulled it out. On it was a picture: green and blue, punctuated by macaroni. He stood for a moment, trying to recollect the night before. Had he tidied this yesterday? Before he went to bed? He couldn't remember.

The music was annoying him now. It was stopping him thinking clearly. He turned and pushed the power button on the speaker. He needed silence to focus his thoughts. He perched on the edge of the desk and stared around the room, trying to bring to mind the evening before.

Across the room, at eye level, he noticed a brown envelope toward the bottom of one of the piles of paper. About a quarter of the envelope was sticking out toward him. He got the feeling that it was somehow trying to attract his attention, so went over for a closer look. He vaguely recognised it, and lifted the paper on top so he could slide the envelope out. It was sealed. He turned it over and saw, in neat print on the front, 'R S

Perkins'. This was bizarre. He tore the packet open and pushed his hand into the darkness. His fingers felt the contents, and from inside he retrieved three small books. Two blue. One red.

He suddenly felt a little dizzy. A little sick. He steadied himself on the piano for a moment, and then turned and managed to reach the chair before he lost his balance completely.

It was dark when Ian awoke. He lifted his head from his forearm, which had been resting on the desk, and saw three small books piled neatly atop one another on the surface in front of him. His neck cracked as he stretched. He felt groggy. His shoulders ached. He lowered his head again – this time resting his chin on his forearm – and stared out of the window. The moon was visible high in the sky through the little panes of glass.

It was then he heard the sound. It was hard to describe. Not quite a bang, more a thud. The sound of something falling. He rubbed his eyes and sat upright. Silence. He pulled his sleeve back and pushed the little red button on the side of his watch. The blue light that illuminated the face was the only light in the room. It was just after ten.

He heard the noise again. A thump. Like a heavy book being dropped onto carpet. It seemed to be coming from above.

He switched on the desk light and stood. Then he counted to three in his head and pulled open the study door. The hall was dark, apart from the moon's silvery rays through the small panes of glass in the front door. He felt around the corner and pushed the light switch. A moment's pause then, thankfully, the ceiling light burst into life. Dull at first. It would brighten over the next minute or two.

He paused again. Then he began a whispered count, forming the first word as he breathed out. *One*. His heart beat quickly. Breathe in. *Two*. Then, as he breathed out again: *Three*. He pushed his head out into the hall and looked around. Nothing. Feeling a miniscule increase in confidence, he moved his foot forward.

Then he was in the hall. He stood for a moment, his back against the triangular-shaped wall where the bannister disappeared right above him, and listened. If he heard the noise again, he could get to the front door before whoever it was could get down the stairs. His dilemma was what to do when he got outside. Rachel had the car, and it was a long way to run to anywhere at all.

He tried to silence his breathing. He knew that he would have found this situation difficult at the best of times, but after his unexpected sleep, it seemed so much worse. He felt fuzzy, which wasn't helping his decision-making. Maybe there was nothing there. Maybe he had just heard a random and totally explainable noise. Everything was quiet now. The only sound he could hear was the fizz of electricity travelling through the old wiring into the now-bright lightbulb. It was okay. It was nothing.

He took a step forward, moving away from the wall, and arched his neck to look upstairs. He couldn't see. It was still black up there. He waited for a moment, and then took two deliberate paces to his right. Stopping at the bottom of the stairs, he listened. Nothing. He flicked the switch and the landing light illuminated. He peered up the stairs at the mustard-coloured glass lampshade that encircled it. It was a light fitting he had promised to change so many times. When Rachel was pregnant, she had complained that it was difficult to make her way around the landing with such a dim light and she was worried she may fall down the stairs. He cursed himself for his indolence. The landing light was no better than candlelight.

He rubbed his eyes and stared into the gloom, trying to see into the shadows that fell on the walls. And there it was again. A thud. Heavier this time. It came from the landing area to his right, toward Rachel's room. Maybe Harry's.

Ian stood rigid, trying to consider his next move. The noise reminded him of Harry leaving his bed – the sound of two little feet landing at the same time on carpet; a climb to halfway down the bunkbed ladder, and then a jump onto the softness beneath him. The noise was ingrained in Ian's memory. When Harry was smaller, he used to climb from his bed at all times during the night. It happened so often that when Ian and Rachel were sitting in the lounge in the evening watching television, Ian would imagine that he had heard it. He'd roll his eyes, give an 'I'll go' signal to Rachel and get off the sofa. Then, when he reached the hall, he'd find it empty, there'd be no sign of Harry. But on some nights, the little boy would appear in the space

87

Ian was staring into now, complaining that he couldn't sleep because of monsters or ghosts or some other creature he had heard about.

Ian backed up slightly, shuffling a few feet nearer to the front door – his escape route. He half-expected to hear the handle of Harry's bedroom door squeak as ten little fingers heaved with all their might to pull it open. But there was silence. The only sound was the excitable electricity. And Ian's breathing. Realistically, he considered, it was likely that his mind was playing tricks on him. Just like before. There was nothing upstairs. There was nobody in the house.

Or perhaps there was.

Maybe Rachel had returned whilst he'd been asleep. This was possible. And in their current predicament, it wouldn't surprise him at all if she'd returned, not said a word and taken herself and Harry off to bed. Yes, this was likely. He was about to shout up the stairs when he realised that if they were there, his shouting would only wake them, and from experience he knew it would take forever to get Harry back to sleep.

He edged past the bottom of the stairs and pushed open the door to the lounge. It made a long, high-pitched sound, and then cracked as the hinge strained. He rushed over to the window and leaned on the windowsill, craning his neck to see whether the car was on the drive. Huge raindrops flew toward him, hitting the window and exploding before escaping like precious jewels down the glass. They reminded him of the bird. Relentlessly hitting. Again. And again. Large bubbles of water had collected on the window, making it almost impossible to see. Ahead of him he could make out the black outline of the tree swaying in the wind. The rain battered the window, as if it was being thrown in giant handfuls from the branches of the tree itself. An ambush, purposely obscuring his view. It was no good, he couldn't see out to the driveway. It was too wet. Too dark.

He walked slowly back across the room to the hall, rolling his feet from heel to toe, so as not to make a noise. At the very moment he reached the bottom of the stairs, he heard the noise again. A dull thud. Then nothing. He took a deep breath and put his hand on the bannister. Much as he didn't want to, he was going to have to tackle this. Deal with the situation. Something he never did, apparently – well, that's what Rachel had said recently, more times than he could remember.

He gingerly climbed the first two steps and then thought better of his strategy. The sound of his heart and the intermittent creaking of the stairs was only making the situation worse. So many times, he had shouted at the lead character in the horror films he loved, telling them what they should do when presented with by an unknown noise in a large, empty house. On a rainy night. In the middle of nowhere. Now, ironically, he was the lead character, and he had a choice: to walk into the unknown, or not. For once, he decided to take his own advice.

"Rachel! Harry!" he shouted at the top of his voice. "Are you there?" He was shaking; he didn't care whether he woke them or not now.

He repeated his call as he made his way up the stairs, pulling himself up by the bannister as if engaged in some kind of tug of war. He purposely stamped his feet down on each step. If there was a stranger upstairs, they would hear him, and the noise he was creating would let them know he wasn't afraid. Of course he was, but that didn't matter. The stranger didn't know that. He reached the top of the stairs and switched on the bathroom light to brighten the landing.

Adrenalin surged through his body. He moved quickly, with purpose. Three paces. He pushed opened Harry's door, allowing it to bang against the wall behind. The palm of his hand hit the switch and the room was flooded with light. There was Harry's bunkbed, his desk beneath it, scattered with Toy Story figures, felt-tips and scribbled sheets of paper. Ian climbed the bottom rung of the ladder to make sure Harry wasn't hidden under the duvet above. He wasn't. The covers and pillows were straight. Unslept in.

He glanced around the room. There was nowhere else to hide. He was relieved; the room was empty. He backed out of the room and then moved along the landing, past the airing cupboard. He reached Rachel's door and turned the handle and pushed. The door didn't move. He tried again and pushed with his shoulder. There was a slight movement at the top, but it stayed firm at the bottom. The door was locked. His breathing increased, and he caught a slight smell of old coffee. The house was so quiet. He could only hear himself.

He got down on his hands and knees so he could see. Attached to the front of the door was an old rectangular brass box that formed the lock. He could see the strip of metal that crossed the gap between the door and frame. He peered into the space where the large brass key would go. He couldn't see anything; it was too dark. He was breathing more quickly now. Sharp breaths, in and out, in and out. He reached into his pocket and pulled out his phone. Using the torch, he was sure he could see the end of a key on the other side.

He stood and knocked on the door, calling his wife's name and waiting momentarily for a response before hitting the door again.

She must be in there.

"Rachel," he cried. He was getting desperate. His fists pounded on the door. Still there was no answer.

He waited a moment, hoping for some inspiration, for somebody, somewhere, to tell him what to do. Nothing.

So he banged again, this time more furiously.

Nothing.

He took a step backwards and then raced forwards. His shoulder collided with the door and he heard the cracking of wood. The door moved slightly. He continued to call Rachel's name. Again, he flew into the door. And again. He wiped the sweat from his forehead and hit the door again.

And then it was open, and his momentum carried him on and he fell, crashing into the small table to the left of his wife's bed. The lamp fell and then stopped in mid-air, hanging by its taut wire over the edge of the table. A small silver frame containing a picture of Harry landed on the floor next to Ian.

He rested for a second, then pulled himself up and sat on the floor with his back against the bed. He looked around the room. It was dark, lit only by moonlight and the dismal mustard colour from the landing. The room was small. A bed. A bedside table. A television. There wasn't even enough room for a wardrobe. There was nowhere to hide. The room was empty. Through the window he could see the dark branches of the tree waving like a crooked hand in the distance.

Ian stood and exhaled, long and constant, as if he was being breathalysed. He collected the piece of brass and collection of screws that had landed on the carpet near the door. There was no key. He carefully picked up the thin splinters of broken wood and placed them in the bin. The lock would be fixed tomorrow, before Rachel and Harry returned. He switched on the light and took one last look around the room.

Definitely empty.

He turned off the light and walked onto the landing.

And then he heard a thud.

Exactly the same as before.

It seemed to have come from the study beneath him.

TWELVE

Ian intended to spend the whole of Sunday in the study. There was so much paperwork to get through, and the strange noises the previous night had inspired him to stop his constant procrastination and just get on with it. In fact, he had repeated this mantra out loud as he had dressed, during his usual early-morning conversation with himself. And so he was awake by seven and in the kitchen by seven fifteen, a large coffee his assistant. There was no time to shower this morning; he needed to get straight on with it.

The night before, after hearing the last thud, he had raced around the house, switching on every light and shouting at the top of his voice. He had been in every room, and checked every cupboard and possible hiding place. When he was content that the sounds were simply his imagination, he had finally gone to bed, his nervousness dissipated, his shouts and cries having released the fear inside him. There had been no more thuds, no more bangs after that. He had fallen asleep quite quickly, though his dreams had been heavy with childlike screams.

He collected his coffee and walked over to the range table. The sun burst in through the French windows, warming him. Much as he wanted to watch the day ahead unfold from his usual seat, he knew that he couldn't. He would just stand for a few more moments and then begin his work. It was beautiful outside. The dew was coloured by the sun, so the garden was covered in a million tiny golden beads, shining and rippling like a gilded stream. He wanted to wade out into it; feel it surround his body and its gentle current carry him away.

He took a sip of his coffee and placed it down on the range table, next to the box he had converted into a coffin for the bird. He picked it up, surprised by how light it was. He prised open the lid, and removed the thin layer of kitchen paper. He was shocked to find the box empty. The rest of the white paper was still in place, and he could vaguely see the indentation where the bird had lain.

He put the box down on the table and eased into a chair alongside it. He stared for a moment. It didn't make sense. In fact, nothing in the last few days, weeks, even months made sense. He ran his fingers through his hair, grabbed a clump with each hand and pulled, as if trying to tear it from his head. Then, using his fist, he rained blow after blow onto the box until it was flattened. He got up and walked over to the bin. He pressed the pedal, the lid flipped open excitedly, and he slammed the remains of the box into the bin.

Too much time had been wasted collecting information and doing nothing with it. It was vital he got to the truth. He had to make this situation stop. And proving his theory was the only way he could begin to contemplate his life improving. He carried his coffee through to the study.

None of the papers appeared to have moved during the night, which was pleasing. Everything seemed to be where it should be – in the shambolic way he had left it. He switched on the radio and began by collecting a pile of paperwork from the piano and placing it on the desk. Judging by the height, there were probably around two thousand sheets in that pile alone to scan through.

He picked the first sheet from the top of the pile and studied it. It was a printout from his computer; an old, grainy picture of Cobweb Cottage. The quality was extremely poor. In front of the cottage stood a family of four, two adults and two children. He assumed they must be some distant relatives. The tree was out of shot, but it made its presence felt by casting a shadow over the top of the house. Dark, thin, spiky fingers crept up the roof toward the chimney. One of the upper windows was obscured by a white burst of light, which Ian assumed must have come from the sun. The writing beneath stated that the photograph was taken at some time in the late nineteenth century. He took a Post-it note and scribbled 'Cobweb Cottage' on it. He stuck it to the paper and placed the paper to his left, on the corner of the desk.

Like almost all the papers, the next sheet was another printout, this time from an archived notice of death. Ian held it up in front of him. The announcement had been made by Louisa Perkins regarding her son, Stephen. He had 'tragically passed' on 16 May 1980. He would be missed by his family. Ian went to the printer and made a copy. On the original, he highlighted Stephen's name. On the copy, he did the same for Louisa. Then he carefully wrote out a Post-it for each of their names and stuck it to the front. He began a new pile on the desk for each of them.

For the next hour, he made his way through the papers, scanning each sheet and extracting the information he needed. The papers were in no discernible order, just random sheets collected over many months. Where necessary, he would copy and highlight the names. Some names he recognised. His father, Paul; his uncle, Stephen; and his brother. But many were names of Perkins that meant nothing to him. There were also, of course, plenty of names that weren't Perkins, those family members who had been married off or those people who had – in hindsight rather stupidly – married into the family.

There was only enough room on the desk for sixteen separate stacks, and Ian had soon run out of room. If he was going to organise everything and construct a family tree then he needed more space. Much more.

He decided to remove the piles of paperwork from the piano. He lifted each carefully and loaded them on top of one another against the wall. It was no exaggeration to say that if it had been possible to stack them one on top of the other, the pile would have been taller than Ian. Instead, he separated them into four smaller towers. They reminded him of a city skyline – a slightly skewed, crumbling city skyline.

He continued his work, copying, highlighting, adding to existing piles and making new ones on the piano where necessary. The paperwork on his desk began to rise, the small dossier on each family member now in some kind of order. By early afternoon, he had completed the reorganisation of the original stacks of paperwork. He was pleased with his work. This was the most driven he had been for a number of months. At last it seemed like he was getting somewhere.

He looked over at the papers against the wall and smiled, shaking his head slightly. There was a hell of a long way to go. Like digging the foundations of a house, the brief feeling of achievement was soon replaced by a realisation of the sheer amount of work ahead to have somewhere to shelter.

After a quick sandwich, Ian was back in the study. He happened across the little blue diaries and searched through their pages for something, anything, that would help. The two years' worth of information was much the same as in the red diary: mundane. The weather. An evening meal.

Slightly disheartened, he walked over to the desk and scanned the neat piles of paper. The tallest belonged to Henry Perkins, his grandfather. Ian picked up the papers and sat back in the chair. He removed the Post-it from the front page and read. It was a newspaper article printed from the online archive site of the local newspaper, *The Low Mill Messenger*. Where the original photograph would have been was a grey box with a cross in the top corner. Underneath, the caption read 'Henry Perkins, local farmer'. The font was tiny and the article wasn't correctly formatted. Sentences began and ended abruptly halfway across the page, making it difficult to read. Ian carefully made his way through the text.

The article told the story of the death of his grandfather,

Henry, in 1951. He had been found dead in the fields behind Cobweb Cottage. From what Ian could understand, Henry's body was recovered from the edge of a nearby stream. Ian thought for a moment. He could picture the scene. Yes, the stream was about a mile and a half away from the back of the cottage. He and Stuart used to play there when they were young. He had a vague memory that their father once took them there. It was only a few hundred metres from the woodland area where most of their adventures unfolded. He read on.

His grandfather's body was discovered crushed beneath an upturned tractor. It was clear that he was dead when the small search party of farmworkers found his body. Seemingly, it had been a 'tragic accident'. The article confirmed that Henry Perkins left behind a wife, Louisa, and two sons, Paul and Stephen.

Ian fumbled around in the top drawer of his desk and pulled out his pad. The pages were filled with his scrawled handwriting, notes that he had hurriedly made when he first began this task a few months earlier. He flipped through the pages until he found a blank page. On it, he scrawled down the vital information he had just read: his grandfather's name, his date of death and the words 'tragic accident'.

Ian continued through the pile, reading different articles about Henry's death. Most repeated the same information, but from time to time Ian would find a tiny nugget of extra information: the tractor was made by John Deere; Henry had a fractured skull; the funeral would be at St Mary's Church.

Eventually, near the bottom of the papers, he found an article that was more recent than the others, dated a few months after the reports on Henry's death. The coroner's report had been issued. After a short hearing, he had concluded that Henry's death was indeed an accident. Ian placed the pile back neatly on the desk and stretched. That was enough for one day.

An hour later, Ian found himself by the stream. It was a beautiful summer evening and a gentle breeze ran through the trees, reflecting green diamonds on the water's surface. The sun had seemingly also had enough for the day, and was lowering quietly behind the horizon. Ian lay back on the small incline that fell toward the stream. He gripped clumps of grass between his fingers, idly pulling them from the ground, and stared at the sky, imagining that he was lying where his grandfather had been found.

It had been a good day. He was pleased with his progress, more so than on any other day since he'd begun his journey for the truth. He wished that Rachel would get involved; maybe if she did, that would pull them closer together again. On the occasion that he had asked her to help, she had momentarily flicked through the papers and then excused herself. She'd shown no interest since then. Her help would be invaluable. She was organised, intelligent. She would certainly help solve the mystery sooner, and that could only be in both of their best interests. She was certainly interested in the television programme where celebrities traced their family history. Maybe now he had begun to sort the endless paperwork into some semblance of order she may be inspired to help. Ian resolved to ask her again to help when she returned later that night.

He sat up.

A pink haze flickered across what was left of the sun. He watched the stream for a moment, the flow of water breaking around the rounded stones that stuck out through the surface. He listened carefully, hoping to hear whispered secrets in the trickle of the water.

As Ian approached the cottage, he saw Rachel at the window. She was standing at the kitchen sink. He climbed on top of the small stone wall and hopped down into the garden. He waved. She didn't return the gesture. Perhaps she hadn't seen him. He strode across the lawn, admiring the lines which ran perfectly straight, in line with the disused barn. The lawn came to an end at the kitchen window. Rachel was gone.

He took his shoes off and pushed open the French doors. The kitchen was empty. He shouted his wife's name. No answer. He glanced at his watch; it was past Harry's bedtime. No doubt she'd be upstairs with him. He quenched his thirst with a large gulp of water directly from the tap, and wiped his mouth on his sleeve. He shouted to Rachel again. No answer. This was confusing.

He moved into the hall, continuing his shout. The study door was open, the light off. He was distracted by a sound coming from upstairs and walked to the bottom of the stairs.

He shouted Rachel's name yet again. This time there was a response. It was muffled, and he couldn't hear what she had said. He stared up the empty stairs.

"Rachel, are you up there?" he asked. He heard the click of her bedroom door.

"Yep. What's up?"

"I was just checking it was you."

She leaned over the bannister, her wet hair dangling like vines over the edge. Ian saw black half-circles beneath her eyes.

"Well, who else would it be, Ian?" she snapped.

He ignored her question. He didn't think it required an answer.

"Is Harry asleep?" he said, reducing his words to a whisper.

Rachel stared at him.

"Yes, Ian. He's asleep," she said firmly.

"Right," said Ian. He knew that tone.

He was disappointed that he hadn't returned from his walk in time to see his son. It was late, though, and he figured Harry had probably fallen asleep on the long journey back. Ian climbed the first step – he'd just pop his head around the door to say goodnight.

"Don't," said Rachel.

Ian looked at her.

"Just don't," she said, turning away.

He stared into the space she had just vacated. Then she reappeared. "Oh, and while we're at it, tell me, why do you think it's okay to break into my room while I'm away?"

"I, er –"

"What exactly did you think you'd find in there?"

"Nothing, I heard –"

She was gone.

Back into her bedroom.

Ian wanted to continue the conversation, but he stopped himself shouting after her. He didn't want to wake Harry. That would only provide the spark in an already explosive situation. Instead, he turned and went into the lounge. He slumped down on the sofa and pressed the button on the remote. The television made a space-age whooshing noise as it came on. The programme was about the palaces and country getaways of the British monarchy. He pulled a cushion behind his head and stared at the screen.

THIRTEEN

The land that Cobweb Cottage was built on had been acquired by the Perkins family in the late eighteenth century. Originally, the Perkins family lived in an old stone barn approximately four miles away from where Cobweb Cottage now stood. Over the next seventy years or so, the ownership of the land changed as it passed from generation to generation. At some time in the middle of the nineteenth century somebody decided that the family should move to a different location on the sprawling two hundred acres of farmland.

And so, that's what the family did. The location was chosen and the property that is now Cobweb Cottage was built. The stone barn that had been the old family home was left unused for many years, and then one night a storm partially claimed the roof. After that, it didn't take long for the weather to destroy the interior. Each generation since has sworn to reroof it or to renovate it or to simply clear it out for storage purposes. Presently, it continues to be four stone walls standing in the middle of a field with only each other for company.

Whoever it was who made the decision to move location, they made the right choice. The new location is far better than the position of the old barn. Here, the property sits in a flatland of fields, drenched by sunlight seemingly from all directions all day long. The road at the front of the cottage provides good access to the nearest village. At the bottom of the garden, over the fields, is a beautiful stream that travels endlessly as far as the eye can see. And, perhaps most importantly, there is nobody else around for miles and miles, no other properties overlooking the cottage. Splendid isolation.

The cottage was only given its present name in the early twentieth century. Apparently, it was named after the condition of the interior when the next generation moved in. Every surface, every picture rail, every corner was covered in cobwebs. Prior to that, the cottage didn't really have a name. There was a sign at the end of the drive, near where the white wooden fence sits today. The sign was cut from an oval piece of oak, the bark remained around its edges. It hung from two small chains that were attached at either end. Hand-painted in white, it simply read 'Perkins'. Whoever wrote it didn't have the imagination to even add the word 'Farm' to the end, or at a push, 'Manor'.

The land, outbuildings and the cottage itself are all held in a family trust. The trust was drafted many, many years ago. Although the trust deed itself is a huge document, written by hand in black ink on beautiful, thick ochre paper, in many ways what it contains is ultimately very simple.

The Trust is for the benefit of the eldest surviving son of George Perkins. If the son has died, the Trust's assets pass to his children. If the eldest surviving child dies without children, the assets simply pass to his eldest sibling. And it is for that very reason that Ian Perkins now finds himself living in the cottage.

The story goes that one of the reasons the location for the property was chosen was its situation in a clearing – a wide expanse of flat ground with no trees for more than a mile in any direction. It was possible to stand at any window and see nothing but open space. As a consequence, the cottage was never going to sit in the darkness of shadows.

A year or two after the property was built, a child was born into the Perkins family. A little girl. Sadly, just three years later, she passed away. On the morning of the funeral, the child's father was standing outside the cottage, waiting for the funeral cortège to arrive. As he watched for the steady flow of horses and carriages to appear in the distance, he noticed a small shoot. It was right in the centre of the large expanse of cropped, slightly yellowed grass, which in those days led right to the edge of the road – a small shoot, breaking through the soil, standing tall above the grass. He walked over and knelt beside it. It was about a foot in height. A handful of large, five-pronged green leaves came from the thin stalk. At the top, tiny, unopened red leaves were ready to unfurl.

As the father held the plant in his hand, ready to pull it from its roots, he heard a voice. He looked over his shoulder, expecting to see his wife. But he was alone, kneeling in the middle of an empty garden. Quietly at first, he heard horses' hooves and the rumblings of the carts, one of which would carry the body of his daughter to the church. And then, distinctly, he heard the voice again. An infant's, as light and breathless

105

as the wind itself that day. She whispered simply, "Leave me here. Always."

The father let go of the small shrub and stood. He wiped the tears from his eyes with a white handkerchief, and pushed it back into his pocket. He looked up to the house, hoping that nobody had seen.

FOURTEEN

Ian turned over and opened his eyes. The television continued its broadcast: the morning news. It took him a moment to get his bearings, and then slowly he turned his head toward the ceiling. The side of his neck hurt, and he pulled himself up to a sitting position so he could massage it. The clock in the bottom corner of the television screen told him it was 8:56 a.m. Above it was a bright yellow picture of the sun. Obscuring the sun, in gaudy orange text, were the words 'Wake Up Britain'.

It was nearly nine o'clock. Rachel and Harry would have left by now. He was annoyed that they hadn't woken him to say goodbye.

He rubbed his neck again. It was sore. He moved his head from side to side to loosen his neck, his movements drawing an invisible infinity symbol in the air. As he did so, he could hear little cracking sounds as the muscles stretched. He nestled back onto the sofa and listened to the television. A lady was reading the day's local news. There had been a huge fire at a local mattress company. The building had collapsed. Three were missing. A local campaigner was furious over the speed at which cars travelled past the village infant school. She wanted speed bumps installing. The lollipop lady shared her opinion.

Ian switched off the television and lay in silence. The house was silent too. The only sounds came from the birds outside, which appeared to have extremely urgent news to impart. He had never heard them twitter and warble so much. He listened, imagining that he could somehow work out what it was they were saying. It was unlikely they wanted speed bumps too.

About half an hour later, he finally dragged himself from the sofa. He had concluded that it wasn't possible to interpret the birdsong, and anyway, his daydream had been rudely interrupted by a booming theme tune for some programme about burglary in Britain. He rolled from the sofa and made his way into the kitchen. He poured himself a glass of orange juice and stood at the kitchen window for a moment. Yet another beautiful day. The weather had been strange recently, he thought. Eternally bright. Eternally warm. It seemed to be some kind of sign. It was the type of day that inspires a person, a reminder of how spectacular the world is – and life itself. He smiled and began humming. Today was going to be a good day. There was much to do.

The sight that greeted him in the study was enough to instantly extinguish all pleasure he felt. The room was in total disarray. All the careful piles of paperwork had been swept from the piano onto the floor. There was paper everywhere. The desk was the same. The neat stacks had been pushed together, all converging into one mess in the middle. It reminded him of a bonfire. An A4 bonfire. The piles of paperwork that he had stacked against the wall – the ones he had intended to begin sorting that day – were similarly tipped over onto the floor. He could barely see the carpet beneath.

For a few moments he just stood and stared.

There was little else he could do.

And then he felt a tiny spark of anger. Seconds later, it had grown into a full-blown forest fire. Why would Rachel destroy all the work he had put in? What did she have to gain from it? It wasn't as though she could be jealous of the time he spent in the study; he had suggested a thousand things that they could do together. A walk. A trip to the local pub. A meal out. Jeez, he'd even suggested a holiday abroad. Each suggestion had been greeted with a shake of the head, or a simple "no". In fact, he would gladly have given up any time in the study to spend some time with her. To do this, for no good reason? Well, that was it: he'd had enough. He wasn't going to keep his mouth shut this time.

He went into the hall in search of his phone, which he eventually found in-between the cushions of the sofa.

He called Rachel.

Straight to voicemail.

He left a message asking her to ring him.

He called again and left a further message.

Back in the study, Ian got down on his hands and knees and began collecting the papers. He wasn't going to be defeated, and Rachel's act of wanton destruction had further ignited him. He spent the majority of the day sweeping up papers from the floor and the desk and the piano. He flicked through them, one by one, and reorganised them back to the way they had been the day before.

Ian was sitting cross-legged on the floor when Harry entered the room. His little face was shining, his skin slightly browned by the endless days of sun. He was beaming. As soon as he saw his father, his eyes widened and he rushed over to Ian, who pulled him close. Ian *needed* to hold him. It seemed like forever since he had last seen Harry. His hair smelled of shampoo, his coat of fire. Ian recoiled and loosened his grip.

"Phew! Your coat smells," he said. "Where have been?"

"At nursery, Daddy. Silly!"

"I know that, but when have you been near a fire?"

"There's no fire at nursery, Daddy."

"Why does your coat smell of fire then?"

"Because" – he screwed up his face to show he was thinking – "of fire, Daddy."

Ian thought it best to leave the conversation there; he was unlikely to get any type of sensible response. He made a mental note to ask Rachel later.

"Okay, sweetheart," he said, putting an end to any more talk of fire. "So what happened at nursery today?"

"Er, noth...ing" – he drew out the words – "re...ally. I suppose you could say."

Ian laughed. "I suppose you could."

"So, Daddy, more messy work today?"

"Yeah. I'm tidying it all up today."

"Doesn't look too tidy today, really," Harry said, looking at the stacks of paper near the wall. They were taller than him.

"I know. It will be later, though."

Harry held Ian's finger and smiled. The afternoon sunlight lit up his blue eyes with a thousand colours. Ian pulled him close again. "I love you, son," he said.

Harry used both his hands to push against Ian's shoulder, prising the hug apart.

"Right, I'm going now," he declared joyfully.

Ian let go. Harry tottered toward the door.

"Harry," Ian said.

Harry turned to face him. His eyes were wide as he waited for the next sentence.

"I love you."

"I love you too, Daddy. Forever and a mile."

Ian laughed, and then Harry was gone and tears gathered in Ian's eyes. Tears of anger. Of frustration. Of sadness. Of wanting the family to be back to how they were. He wiped his eyes and told himself that crying wasn't going to help. Only one thing was going to help, and it was in the papers that surrounded him in every direction. He stood, selected the loudest, heaviest-sounding record he could find and turned the volume up.

As darkness fell upon the room, the papers were almost back to how they had been when Ian left them the day before. He was exhausted. The backs of his knees hurt from kneeling. The fronts of his knees hurt from kneeling. His back ached. His neck was stiff. The carpet had reappeared and he laid back, crucifixion style, on the floor. Tomorrow he would begin again. And he would get to the truth, no matter what it took.

He stood and rummaged through the various mugs and jars on the shelves around the room; he knew it was in one of them. He clutched a handful of pens and poked his fingers in the bottom of each container. Most were either empty or contained a few paperclips or treasury tags. A pencil sharpener. An eraser. A coin. Then he remembered where he had put it. It was in the piano stool.

He walked across the room and opened the lid. There it was, just where he remembered, beneath the unused 'Learn to Play Guitar' books. The small silver key.

He smiled and walked into the hallway, pulling the door closed behind him. He locked it and tried the handle, and when the door wouldn't open he safely stowed the key in his pocket.

FIFTEEN

The family never spoke of Uncle Stephen again. After the funeral, they silently returned home and the subject was considered closed. The following morning, Ian asked a question about the previous day and the look from his father told him that even the name of Uncle Stephen was taboo. Privately, Ian also tried to speak to Stuart about the funeral, but he was as resolute as his father, greeting Ian's question with a firm rebuke: "You heard Dad. Never talk about it again. Okay?"

And Ian didn't.

And nothing was ever the same again.

The death of Uncle Stephen changed Stuart. It was as if somewhere in the corridors of Stuart's mind he had happened upon a previously unopened door. When he pushed it open and entered, it shut firmly behind him and that's where he remained, trapped for the rest of his life. And the room was permanently dark.

The days of adventures – innocently playing in the surrounding fields and woodlands – were as good as over. Of course, the boys did continue to play (Mum didn't want them "under her feet"), but it was never the same. The make-believe quests they created to slay dragons or eliminate marauding Indians would always end in the same conversation initiated by Stuart. About death. About a family curse. About how things were hopeless now.

As the brothers grew older, their father expected them to help on the farm. Each day after school, they would make the two-mile walk home across the fields: a beautiful golden-green walk in the summer, a slow, thick, sludgy trudge in the winter. Each day they passed the exact spot that Uncle Stephen's car had been found, where his fractured body had lain until it was discovered the next morning.

Not once did they speak about it.

When they got home, they quickly changed out of their school uniforms and walked down to the bottom of the garden, where their father was waiting for them. The engine of his tractor seemed to splutter and groan in unison with noises their father made. Always angry. Always impatient. Despite the speed with which Ian managed to clamber aboard, it was never quick enough. He could always be assured of a tut, or a look of annoyance. Once they were both in the tractor, Dad would take them to wherever it was on the farm that needed work. There was always something to do. Fences to fix. Holes to dig. Seeds to sow.

Stuart appeared to enjoy the work, and he stayed close to Dad at all times. Ian would stand watching Stuart watching their father constantly, almost attached to his side, as if he sensed that one day, in the passing of a simple second, Dad would no longer be there. And Stuart was, of course, correct. But his behaviour suggested that the simple second was not too far away.

It was Stuart's sixteenth birthday and the two boys had taken the walk home from school at a more excitable pace than usual. Ian had made Stuart laugh on more than one occasion, which was unusual nowadays. Ian put it down to the anniversary.

They kicked off their shoes and threw down their school bags in the hall. Their mother appeared in the kitchen doorway and informed Stuart to go and work on the farm as usual. He would receive his gifts when he returned. He nodded his dutiful acceptance, and he and Ian went and changed.

Moments later they were in the kitchen. Ian pushed open the French doors. Dad was waiting on the tractor just on the other side of the stone wall, as always. He was staring into the distance at something unknown, as always.

Stuart reached the tractor first, Ian moments behind. Their father turned to greet them at the very last minute. Ian wondered what he was staring at.

"Happy birthday, son," said Dad.

"Thanks, Dad," said Stuart, eagerly climbing up into the cabin. Ian shuffled into the half-seat just behind them.

"Come on," said Dad, "I've got something to tell you about."

The tractor chugged into action and Dad turned it to the left, heading towards the fading sun.

"Here we are," said Dad, pulling the tractor to a stop at the top of a slight incline. He seemed slightly excited; like a child about to share a secret. This was unusual.

Dad jumped down from the cabin clutching a plastic bag in his hand. Ian and Stuart climbed down the metal rungs and followed quickly behind.

"Sit," Dad instructed, pointing to the grass.

Stuart was on the grass in seconds. Ian sat alongside, a few feet away. There was just room for their father to squeeze in between them. The three were sitting on a small grassy slope that led down to a stream. Dad opened the plastic bag and pulled out three yellow cans. He passed one to Stuart and kept the other two for himself.

"Beer?" said Stuart, smiling.

Dad nodded. "The best. Boddingtons."

Ian must have pulled some kind of face, because Dad said to him, "Sorry, son, another two years."

Ian watched as Dad pulled the ring pull and a creamy liquid emerged from the opening, curling over the edge of the can like a white slug. Dad smiled and sipped the froth before it dripped from the end of the can, using his tongue up the length of the can to ensure he didn't miss any. He wiped his mouth and let out a satisfied "Aah".

Stuart opened his can, and liquid burst from its container and sprayed his face with cream bubbles.

Ian laughed.

"Piss off," said Stuart.

"Language," said Dad between large gulps of beer.

Stuart tentatively sipped his beer.

A few seconds later, Dad crushed his can in his fist and

opened the second can. He lay back on the grass. "Listen," he said, "now you're sixteen, I want to tell you something."

SIXTEEN

On the kitchen side, partially trapped under a jar of sugar, was a note. Ian snatched it up. It was written in neat, thin, red felt-tip. Before he had even read the first word, he knew what the note was going to say. His eyes scanned the few paragraphs she had written.

She had gone.

It wasn't unexpected.

She would be back.

She needed time.

She had gone to her mother's.

'We'll see you soon. Love, Rachel x' it finished.

Ian laid the note back on the work surface and made a coffee. Then he sat in his usual place, staring down the length of the garden.

Until Harry was born, things had been fine. Fine? Well, okay, things had been good. Yeah, good was a better word. Things had been good. No marriage is one continuous, smooth ride. It couldn't possibly be. There's more than one person involved, each with their own feelings. Yes, Ian concluded, every marriage has its ups and downs. That's normal. And their marriage was no different.

There were little fallouts that lasted through and beyond bedtime. Petty arguments, or things unsaid that irked and left a modicum of resentment between them. Times when at bedtime Ian really didn't feel like putting the toothpaste on Rachel's brush, but still did. When he climbed into bed alongside her without speaking, turned off his bedside lamp and faced away from her. In the darkness, he would lie quietly listening to her breathing, to gauge her anger, whilst his grew with each passing second of silence. All the time he would wish that the stand-off could end and they could get back on with their lives.

But that was all. A small sprinkling of disagreements on an otherwise perfectly baked cake.

They had always envisaged that they would have a family, and they'd planned that Harry would come along perhaps a year or two sooner than he had. They had been married for five years when the time felt right to begin trying for a child. A few months passed without any good news, but it wasn't until a year had passed that Rachel suggested they visit the doctor. From that moment on, what was to become the creation of their precious first child became a wholly medical exercise.

The enjoyment of 'trying' to create a life became carefully orchestrated, a tedious chore. Sex was timed to the hour, the release of eggs the same. Rachel ensured the room was the perfect temperature. They both gave up alcohol. Ovulation predictor kits (or OPKs, as they became known) littered the bedroom. Rachel read somewhere that she should strategically insert a cushion beneath her back to aid the journey of the sperm. She began to take anything that could possibly help, and the kitchen windowsill became a storage area for various herbal potions and tablets. They seemed to have an entire alphabet of vitamins. Ian imagined a quick X-ray of her stomach would show up a graphic not dissimilar to a bubble-gum machine.

But still, as far as creating a life was concerned, nothing happened.

There were one or two false alarms.

But that was all.

Eventually, they were both advised by the local doctor to go for tests. Ian came back completely clear. In fact, his sperm count was uncommonly high. Secretly, this made him feel a little more manly. Rachel went for scans, and on one occasion ink was injected into her to test for any type of blockage in her tubes.

Nothing.

She was fine too.

Another year and a half passed. Sex became a regimented misery, and although the doctors had found no medical reason for their inability to conceive, they decided that they would go for fertility treatment.

More tests. More injections. More visits to the clinic. But they were left with little choice: their marriage was beginning to strain like an overfilled shelf.

And then, just like that, it happened.

Naturally.

Neither could explain why.

Ian celebrated with a beer.

The next six months were an exercise in ensuring that

Rachel came to no harm. The excitement of carrying a child was quickly followed by pure fear. She gave up her job immediately and retreated to their home. Her mother drove over most days simply to sit with her. Rachel watched what she ate. Where she went. Through that winter she only left the house a handful of times, when absolutely necessary. She was terrified that she may catch a cold or a cough and somehow harm the baby.

The scans were all positive. Each time the grainy black-and-white image of Harry was noticeably bigger on the little television set.

Everything was going just fine.

Ian found a job where he could work from home, and a few weeks later the day they had both been waiting for finally arrived. On the predicted due date, Rachel's contractions began at 8am. Ian was there to drive her to the hospital and at 3pm that afternoon Harry Perkins was born. They were home twenty-four hours later.

They lived happily in their small townhouse just on the outskirts of the city. As Harry grew, Rachel got a part-time job at the local school and her mother came over three mornings a week to look after Harry. Ian's job meant that he could also take an active role in caring for his son. It was perfect. They could have done with a little more money, a little more space, but couldn't everyone? Harry was a healthy little boy and life was turning out just the way that Ian and Rachel had hoped. Feeling content was probably an understatement.

And then, in the middle of that summer, they got the news

about Stuart. It came in the form of a letter telling them that they were now legally entitled to occupy Cobweb Cottage. Stuart had no children. The solicitor's letter explained that the trust deed dictated that they were next.

They discussed whether it was a good idea. There was, of course, a certain emotional connection for Ian, something magical about bringing up his son in the same place he'd grown up – regardless of how his childhood there had been. There were wrongs to be righted. This was his opportunity. The acres upon acres of open space and the fresh country air were certainly attractive for them both. Plainly, it was idyllic.

Over the years that had passed, Ian had come to terms with the fact that he'd never live in the cottage. It was something that he'd conditioned himself to ignore. In his early twenties it had rankled him. It seemed so unfair that simply the order you were born in would give you the key to an English paradise or, well, nothing. But as time passed, he simply accepted that these were the rules and there was no changing them. Anyway, Stuart seemed far more equipped and interested in farming the land. He was the one who had put the effort in, and when their father fell ill, Stuart's efforts were, not unreasonably, repaid.

The solicitor told Ian and Rachel that if they declined the opportunity, the right to occupy the property would instead pass to distant relatives, who probably didn't even know that the farm existed. To Ian, this didn't seem right. The history was attached to his bloodline and that of his forefathers.

Ultimately, their indecision over moving came down to three

simple problems. Firstly, Rachel worried that Ian wouldn't be settled in the property knowing the tragedy that had unfolded there. Each and every time he looked out of the kitchen window, he would be greeted by the sight of the large barn that occupied the view to his left. The final place Stuart had seen. Secondly, Ian worried that Rachel wouldn't be able to cope with the significant distance between her and her mother. The third and final problem, though Ian never openly expressed it, was the mere thought of the curse. Whenever he brought it to mind, it would stop him dead and lift the hairs on his arms, instantly chilling him.

A week after the funeral, they made their decision.

Six weeks later they were in Cobweb Cottage.

And they were happy.

Ian was content that not telling Rachel about the curse was the right decision.

SEVENTEEN

"One day," Dad said, stretching his arm wide, in line with the horizon, "the whole farm will belong to you, son."

He put his arm around Stuart's shoulders and took another drink of his beer.

"Really?" said Stuart. The excitement in his voice suggested that he had just been given the best birthday present ever.

He had.

"The whole thing. The buildings, the fields, Cobweb Cottage." Dad turned and pointed. "Even that tractor."

"What about me?" said Ian.

Dad shook his head. "Sorry," he said.

Dad began to tell them the story he had brought them to the stream to hear. He told them that his father had died on the farm when he was just four years old. He could vaguely remember a red-faced man with a mess of ginger hair and a gruff voice, but that was all. He described how after his father had died his mother had taken to wearing black clothes and refused to leave the house. Refused to cook. Refused to do anything. For a while, Dad felt that he and Stephen were looking after their mother and not the other way around. Eventually, Dad's grandfather had taken control and hired people to come and look after the farm. His mother had begun to get better, and a year or two later had married Alan, one of the farmworkers, who moved into Cobweb Cottage with them.

The two boys listened in wonder. They had never heard their father speak so much. Their eyes were locked on Dad, who stared somewhere off into the distance. He continued.

Dad had never really got along with his stepfather, who had little interest in either him or Stephen. For this reason, Dad avoided being in and around the cottage and over the years, with the help of the farmworkers, he had learned how to farm the land. He would spend each day after school working on the land, just like Stuart and Ian did now.

Then, the day after his eighteenth birthday, Dad received an important-looking envelope. It was from a solicitor. At first, he thought he must be in trouble for something, but instead he found that the letter was about Cobweb Cottage and the farm. It was very difficult to understand, and by the time he got to the part signed by a Mr Thornbury-Claremont he was completely confused. He read it again. He admitted that he wasn't very good at reading anyway – he hadn't really tried at school – but he had definitely never seen most of the words before. The letter seemed to say that as from his birthday, he now owned all of the farm.

Dad had folded it up and pushed it into his pocket. He was too scared to mention it anyone, and so the letter remained in his pocket for the next week. After that, when he could find a private moment to himself, he would take the letter out and reread it, trying to understand what it meant.

Soon he received another letter from Mr Thornbury-Claremont. This letter was much shorter, and asked him to make an appointment to go to the solicitor's office and sign some papers. Too frightened to telephone, Dad carried both letters for another week. Then Mr Thornbury-Claremont began ringing the cottage and leaving messages asking Dad to get in touch. In the end, when he felt he might burst under the pressure, Dad asked one of the farmworkers to read the letters for him. The farmworker smiled and confirmed that legally the farm was Dad's.

Two weeks later, Dad signed the papers and the farm was transferred to him.

Dad sighed and looked up to the sky, shaking his head.

"And that's when the real trouble started," he said.

Ian and Stuart looked at their father. His eyes had become glassy. He took another gulp from his beer can. Stuart did the same.

"After the farm was given to me, everything went wrong. Everything."

Dad stared across the fields, then continued his story.

Almost immediately after the farm was transferred, Dad's relationship with his stepfather Alan went from "bloody bad to worse". Alan resented that Dad now owned the farm, and began to make life difficult. Money started to go missing from the farm, and then equipment. A tractor. A Land Rover. Although Dad couldn't prove it, he suspected that his stepfather was

126

behind the thefts, or at least had something to do with them.

Dad spoke to his mother on a number of occasions, but she didn't believe him. Or she didn't want to believe him. Her response was that he "must be mistaken" or that "Alan wouldn't do something like that". It was impossible to get through to her. In a matter of weeks, Dad was shunned. His mother, his brother, his stepfather – none of them spoke to him. If he entered a room, they would leave. The atmosphere in the house was unbearable.

Then one day (he couldn't remember why) an enormous argument had erupted in the front garden of Cobweb Cottage. It was the first time all the family had spoken for nearly a month. Things were said that could never be taken back. Words so cruel and so final that Dad could do nothing more than tell them all to leave the house. Permanently.

At this point, without warning, Alan had attacked Dad. His mother stood by and watched it all happen. Fists and boots were flying in as Dad lay on the floor. The blows were relentless, to his body, to his head, to his face. When Alan finally finished the beating, Dad lay on the floor, staring up at his mother. His face was bleeding and he could barely see out of one eye.

"I knew it would turn out this way," his mother spat. Dad wiped the blood away from his mouth. "You only care about money. Nothing else."

"No," he said.

She leaned down over him. "Your father would be turning in his grave. He would be disgusted by how you've turned out,

Paul."

Dad pulled himself up against the tree. Behind his mother, he saw his brother standing alongside Alan. He could see there was blood on Stephen's knuckles too.

"I knew from the moment you could walk that you'd turn out this way. There was something about you. I knew you'd be just like George. Evil. Pure evil." His mother stood up straight. "Well, you can keep this farm."

Dad had never seen her look so angry. She began walking away. Then she turned and said, "And I hope it's you who's next in line for the curse. I truly do."

"And that was it," said Dad. "They left that day. All three of them."

Ian watched as a solitary tear escaped his father's eye. Dad wiped it away as it reached his cheek and then he finished his beer. Stuart was quiet.

Ian considered what his father had said. It was the first time he had heard him directly mention the curse. Of course, from time to time he had overheard a passing mention of it. But nobody really spoke about it, which meant that he had no real understanding of what it was. And not knowing scared him – enough that it played tricks in his mind when sometimes, in the dead of night, the giant sycamore tree scratched its shadows on his bedroom wall.

"Dad?" Ian asked. He was almost positive that he shouldn't ask the next question.

His father looked at him over the top of the can. His eyes indicated he was listening.

"What is this curse?"

Dad swallowed the beer and burped. "It's a load of rubbish," he said bluntly. "A load of absolute rubbish."

His final word seemed to be very much the final word. Ian was sure that he shouldn't say anymore. His curiosity disagreed.

"But what actually is it, Dad?"

His heart raced in the momentary silence.

"Listen," Dad said, sounding annoyed. He turned to Ian for the first time that afternoon. "Listen carefully. All it is, is a bloody story passed down the family. It's to scare people into doing something they don't want to do. Okay?"

Ian nodded; it seemed like the right thing to do. He wasn't sure what his father meant.

Dad seemed to sense this and continued: "It's like 'if you don't let us stay in this house, you'll be cursed' or 'if you don't lend me a thousand pounds, you'll be cursed' – it's complete and utter rubbish."

Ian nodded. That made much more sense. "But where does it come from?"

Stuart glared at Ian. Ian returned it.

"I'll tell you," said their father.

And so, for the second time that afternoon Dad told them a story. And Ian was amazed by just how much he spoke. It was almost like he had been saving up all these words for the entire sixteen years that Stuart had been alive.

Sometime at the end of the nineteenth century, many years after the sycamore tree first took root in the garden, the house was occupied by a man called George Perkins. He lived there with his wife Annie, their twin sons and youngest daughter, Amelia. Of course, he too was a farmer. And a bully. He was a giant man with giant hands who got his own way by force, if necessary. He farmed the land and sold his produce to those who passed by the house, often whether they wanted it or not.

One day, whilst out in the woods, Amelia found a stray dog. He was skinny and his fur was patchy and worn. He cowered when she first approached him and looked like he hadn't been fed properly for many weeks. After some coaxing, she brought home the dog, and Amelia and Annie cared for him until he was healthy again. They named him Patch.

Annie and the children grew to love Patch, especially Amelia. He quickly became her best friend, happily following her everywhere she went and responding to her every command with an almost exceptional willingness to please. But George hated the dog, because Patch would not do as he said. The dog never followed George's commands, and snapped and snarled every time he entered the room. It almost seemed that Patch did the opposite of what George asked.

Over a number of weeks Patch's disobedience irritated George, until early one morning he snapped. When Amelia came down for breakfast, expecting to be greeted by the dog, he was nowhere to be found. She searched the house. There was no sign of him. She enlisted her mother's help, and they wandered the house together. George sat and ate his breakfast impassively. After exhausting all possible hiding places, Annie and Amelia eventually interrupted George to ask whether he had seen Patch at all that morning. His chair scraped on the stone floor as he pushed it backwards. Then he stood, and walked into the hall. His wife and daughter followed him eagerly. He took them to the lounge window and, without speaking a word, he pointed to the tree in the front garden. Annie saw the rigid body of the dog hanging from the branch. She quickly covered Amelia's eyes. George had been out early that morning, fashioned a noose, collected the dog and hanged it. Patch would not misbehave again.

George left the dog in the tree for many months as a warning, not only to his family but also to those passing by, that it was not a good idea to cross him.

Ever.

A matter of weeks after Patch was hanged, Amelia fell ill. She was exhausted and had trouble mustering the energy to even move. Her mother thought that she was suffering from nervous prostration or something similar, and put her to bed for the weekend. The next day came the terrible fever and constant headache. Amelia rejected any food she was given.

On Monday, Annie summoned the doctor from the nearby village. Though he was nervous to pass the hanging carcass of the dog, he entered the house and saw the little girl. Her

131

skin was grey and she could no longer speak. Her nightgown was wet with sweat. He was confused about her condition but prescribed some medicine for her and suggested she stay in bed until he returned on the Thursday. Her condition seemed to plateau.

Late on the Wednesday night, George went to check on Amelia. He pushed open the bedroom door and walked over to the bed. His daughter was facing the wall. He kneeled alongside the bed and listened for her breathing. He couldn't hear anything, so he pulled her shoulder. Her body flopped in his direction. Her eyes were open. He put his hand on her forehead. Her skin was hot to touch.

The room was quiet. Outside in the fields, he could hear the distant sound of a fox calling. George looked at his daughter, knowing this was the end. Then he thought he heard her breathing – light, almost inaudible breaths. He moved his ear close to her mouth to listen, and he heard her voice.

"You did this," Amelia whispered.

And then her breathing stopped.

And never started again.

"From that day on, people have said that the cottage, the tree, this whole place is cursed."

Ian continued to stare at his father, wondering if he was going to continue the story. He wanted to know what had happened over the next one hundred and twenty years, to the present time. But Dad had stopped speaking. Instead, he was fixated on something in the distance. Ian followed his father's gaze, but aside from the yellow haystacks that looked like golden thimbles on the horizon, he could see nothing.

It was Stuart who broke the silence. His voice was unsteady. "Do you believe it?"

"What did I just say, Stuart? It's a load of old rubbish."

"Do you think that hanging the dog killed the little girl?" asked Ian.

"No. 'Course not."

"Well, why is everyone scared of this curse then?"

"Ian!" said Stuart. His tone was enough for him to leave the words 'shut up' out of the sentence.

"What?" said Ian. "I'm only asking."

"Well, don't."

"Why not?"

"Because..." Stuart paused. "Because Dad said it was rubbish."

"I know. But I'm asking why everyone is scared of it."

"Just shut up now, Ian."

"You."

"I mean it," said Stuart, glaring.

Their father snapped out of his trance. "Listen," he said firmly, "both of you shut up. The curse is rubbish, okay? It's just an old story. That's it."

"But –" Ian said.

"Enough."

"But I –"

"Enough!" Dad shouted. "For Christ's sake, Ian. Know when to bloody stop."

Ian knew he'd better not speak again. But he was confused. It seemed that his father had started a story and then simply left the words hanging in mid-air, like the dog. There was so much more Ian wanted to know, like why Dad had told the story in such a way that it instilled fear whilst being adamant that the curse was rubbish. It didn't make sense. Ian questioned why Dad had even told them the story in the first place. And he couldn't help thinking that his father was, in some ways, quite similar to George Perkins.

Dad crushed the empty can in his hand and picked up the one he had finished earlier from the grass alongside him. He stood up and silently walked over to the tractor. He threw the empties in the small trailer at the back and climbed up into the cabin. The tractor spewed out black smoke as it chugged into life.

Stuart stood and walked to the tractor, purposely allowing the contents of his almost-full can to spill before taking one last drink. He wiped his mouth on his sleeve, and threw the can into the back. It landed with a heavy sound. He climbed in alongside Dad.

Ian stayed where he was. Dad pushed open the little side window and shouted down to him. It was time to leave. Ian just lay staring at the stream. The first blast of the tractor's horn made him jump slightly but he didn't move. He hoped they hadn't seen his slight reaction.

"Ian," his father shouted, "get in. Now."

No movement.

"You've got three seconds…"

Ian only turned when he was sure they couldn't see him anymore. He scrambled up the grass incline and lay on his stomach, peering over the top. He could see dry mud being churned up and spat out from behind the enormous tractor wheels as his father and brother disappeared toward home. Stuart's head bounced in tune with the rugged terrain inside the little red cabin on top.

He stood and stretched. He wasn't sure what, but something had made him not want to get in the tractor for the journey back. He was certainly angry. There was no need for Dad to speak to him in that way. He was only asking questions. And what did Dad expect? He had started it by telling them the story, so why shouldn't Ian ask questions?

He wandered toward the edge of the field and picked up a large stick. He swung it as he walked, scything the overgrown grass that separated the dry, dusty field from the woodland area. He considered going into the trees, but it wasn't as much fun climbing them by himself. He wished that Stuart would spend time with him like he used to, but he had never really been the same since Uncle Stephen had died. He was so much quieter now, so much more serious. He had aged. Childhood was over. Ian wasn't sure why this was – Stuart never even knew Uncle Stephen.

Ian continued his walk until he reached the stone wall and

the back of the cottage was plainly in view. He could see his mother at the sink in the kitchen. He hopped over the stile and onto the lawn, and then ran to the back door and pulled down the handle. She greeted him with a warm smile. Ian pulled at his shoes, trying to remove his feet without undoing the laces. Mum asked where Stuart and Dad were. She hadn't seen any sign of them since earlier that afternoon when the three of them had set out on the tractor. That was more than three hours ago.

Ian explained that he had chosen to walk back and had seen the tractor heading straight over the fields toward the cottage.

Mum looked puzzled. "Are you sure?" she said.

"Er…"

Ian was momentarily distracted by the birthday cake on the table. It was green. In white icing was the number '16', and beneath it was an attempt at the word 'Stuart'. It was barely legible. If Ian hadn't have known whose birthday it was, the word in icing would have offered little in the way of a clue.

"Ian?"

He looked up. "What?"

"Are you sure they were coming back here?"

"Er, yeah. Definitely, Mum. The tractor was heading straight toward the cottage. They should have been back ages ago."

Ian dried himself off. The bath water was the colour of mushroom soup. It was nice to feel clean. He reached his arm into the bath and pulled out the plug. The drain gurgled, making a sound like a creature glugging down the soup like it was the last meal on earth.

He pulled on his pyjamas and went through into his bedroom. It was already dark. He sat on Stuart's old bed, his back to the wall. Even though Stuart had moved into the room next door a few years earlier, he still missed having him there at night. He looked out of the window at the tree. It was perfectly still, its giant, majestic trunk solid. Unwavering. He stared at the lower branches, trying to identify the one that George might have used, but it was too dark to properly make them out. His eyes moved to the top of the tree, where the branches thinned out. He was drawn to the shapes the moonlight cast in-between the twigs. The more he stared, the more he could see.

A broom.

A feather.

A tongue.

Triangular eyes.

Teeth.

He heard the click of his bedroom door, and was relieved to see his mother's face.

"They're back," she whispered.

Ian nodded.

Mum motioned to his bed. Ian leapt across the gap and onto his own bed. He pulled the curtains across fully, making sure that there was no space anywhere – no possibility that he would turn in the night and accidentally see outside. He climbed into his bed and pulled the duvet over him. Beneath the covers, his head faced away from the window.

"Goodnight," Mum said quietly. The door clicked behind her. Ian closed his eyes tightly.

As he tried to sleep he couldn't have imagined just how many times that night the sickly looking little girl would visit his bedside. Nor the loudness of the dog's bark that would come from her mouth.

EIGHTEEN

Ian screwed the note into a ball and dropped it on the kitchen table. Then he thought better and retrieved it and flattened it out on the table. He must have read it ten times. Rachel needed time. She needed to be away from him. Away from the cottage. She still loved him, but there were things that she needed to 'work out'. She asked that he didn't call her for a few days.

He was annoyed that she had taken Harry with her, but understood her reasons. Harry loved seeing Rachel's mum, who would spoil him the whole time they were there. He would enjoy the break, and missing nursery wasn't going to cause any problems. It would be different if he was at school. Ian would, of course, miss Harry, but Rachel said that they would be back soon. And for what it was worth, Ian did have his job to do, whereas Rachel had not managed to return to work for some months now.

Ian retrieved the small silver key from his pocket and posted it into the lock on his study door. If Harry wasn't going to be around for a few days then he may as well throw himself into his research. He resolved to make the best of the situation and finally get to the bottom of the piles of paperwork in his study.

Inside, everything was as he left it – stacks of paper along the piano and on his desk, all in neat piles, each carefully named after one of his predecessors. They varied in size, and as he glanced over them he noticed that Henry Perkins was leading in the information race.

Ian looked toward the wall at three huge, unsorted stacks that awaited him. He sighed. And then laughed. There was nothing to do but get on with the task in hand. It wasn't going to sort itself.

He eyed his rows of records, running his finger along the spines, looking for inspiration. Eventually, he pulled out the dark grey sleeve of Pearl Jam's *Vitalogy* – ah, this brought back memories. Something inside told him this was the right record to listen to. Moments later, the black circle was spinning and the familiar opening drum beats filled the room.

He sat down at the computer and flicked the switch. While it awoke from its hibernation, he thought about what would happen when he had finished his task. He was conflicted. On the one hand, he was desperate to chart the history of the family and to prove once and for all that the curse that so many people had mentioned to him did in fact exist. Conversely, however, he worried what would happen once he had finished. What would he do with his time then? There was some comfort in knowing that he always had something to do. A fall-back. Especially with the situation as it was at home. There was an element of joy in knowing that if he ever felt too alone, he had something to occupy his time. But perhaps solving the mystery would solve everything. Once this was over, he and Rachel could get back to where they'd once been, enjoying their lives together.

Ian wasn't like Stuart had been. He didn't have the skills to farm the land, to repair the broken fences, to harvest the crops, to sort drainage in the fields. Living in the cottage seemed like a lie: he was an impostor, nothing like his forefathers. Except that in his own way he was like them. He too was driven – in his case, driven by the fact that he felt he'd somehow been chosen to solve the family mystery, something that nobody else in his family line had ever done. It was up to him.

He double-clicked the envelope icon and his email inbox appeared. He waded through the usual newsletters that at some stage in the past he had subscribed to, deleting them without reading them. There were three articles submitted by his regular contributors for the film website. He opened the website dashboard and copied and pasted them, then he clicked the button and confirmed that he was happy for them to go live on the website that evening. He didn't bother to read them; he was sure they'd be alright. They were, after all, submitted by people who had been contributing for years. There was also an email from his boss. He read through it. It told him that the quality of the content on the site needed improvement, stating (quite correctly) that Ian hadn't personally contributed a new piece of writing for four weeks. The email was worded very gently, albeit with a veiled feeling of threat.

He swivelled in his chair and looked again at the pile of papers against the wall. He then turned back to the screen and began to type an article. Something new. Something that could keep his boss at bay. After only a few sentences, he could tell that his writing wasn't flowing. Already, the article didn't read well, which was a bad sign. He was hoping he could churn out something generic in fifteen minutes. It wasn't to be. He clicked the cross in the top right-hand corner and closed the document without saving it. It would have to wait.

Padded envelopes containing DVDs and press sheets (explaining the enclosed film's synopsis and actors) seemed to drop through his letterbox each day. At first it was exciting. He was being paid to lie on the sofa and watch films: the perfect job. Not so. The marketing machine of the film distributors wanted their pound of flesh. The constant emails, the phone calls – had he received the film? Had he watched it? What did he think? Could he write about it? Like, soon? He knew there was a drawer full of DVDs in the lounge – he'd watch one of those later and write a review. That ought to keep everyone happy. 'Nothingman' played. Its gentle melodies floated across the room. Ian smiled. It was almost ironic.

He climbed down onto his hands and knees and took the first piece of paper from the first of the large piles against the wall. It was about Henry's funeral. He stood, walked to the piano and placed it on the correct pile. Then he was on the floor again. The next piece was an old archived article about his great-grandfather purchasing a new piece of land. He placed it on the correct pile. Next, a grouping of maps outlining the varying fields and pieces of land around the area. The boundaries of the farm around the cottage were outlined in red ink. He placed it on a pile he had for miscellaneous information.

And then he was on the floor.

Reading.

Standing.

Filing.

Floor.

Repeat.

Read. Stand. File. Floor. Repeat.

About halfway down the pile Ian came across a sealed white A4 envelope. On the front of the envelope was beautiful calligraphic writing. The faded blue ink simply read 'Father's letters'. This looked interesting.

The corners of the envelope were crumpled, and as he opened it the yellow adhesive crumbled and fell away like sand. He pulled out the documents, about twenty sheets of heavy cream-coloured paper, each folded into thirds. Ian knew that he shouldn't read them. Not yet. His task was to sort everything into order based on what related to whom. Only then could he begin to read the papers properly and make sense of them. He knew that reading them as he went along would only hold him up. He'd never finish the job.

But there was something interesting about these documents. As he held them, he felt a light, fluttery feeling rising in his stomach up to his chest, like a thousand birds leaving a tree at the same time, two thousand wings flapping inside him. He felt slightly sick. He imagined this was the feeling experienced by the person holding the winning lottery ticket, watching from their chair and listening as the presenter matched their final number.

He couldn't wait. He opened the first of the documents, bending the paper to stop the creases folding the paper back onto itself. It was a letter on headed paper. The address at the top was Cobweb Cottage, in brown serif lettering.

His eyes scanned to the bottom of the letter. It was signed 'Robert'. He recognised the name – his great-grandfather. Someone Ian had never met. His eyes returned to the top of the letter.

It was addressed simply 'To Father'.

The letter was written in large, expressive cursive, with various letters flamboyantly infiltrating the lines above and below. The content, although interesting, wasn't nearly as exciting as the nervous anticipation. The sender – Robert – was unhappy with his father. There had been an issue with the 'distribution of a barley order' which had 'brought great embarrassment' on him and he hoped that his father 'would have the decency to rectify the situation to his satisfaction'.

Ian skim-read the next letter. Another note from Robert, this time to both his mother and father. In this letter he formally thanked them for the 'oil painting they had presented to him, and the kind consideration therewith'.

He flicked through letters. They were all on the same letterhead, all in the same handwriting, all from the same sender and all to the same recipient – Robert's father, from time to time including his mother. Ian opened the final letter. It was folded three ways just like the others, but was written in red ink. His eyes quickly scanned the top and bottom lines.

'Father.' 'Robert.'

The lettering was wider on this letter. In places the nib of the pen had angrily scratched through the surface of the paper. It read:

Father

I think you know why I am writing. If not, you are more of a fool than I may have ventured to imagine. I know everything about you now and I swear by Almighty God that I will make sure everyone knows of the person you are. I will use every moment until drawing my last breath to tell the world what you have done and how your boundless cruelty has cursed this family.

Robert

Ian smiled. This was the first time since he'd begun that somebody had mentioned the curse in writing. It had now become real. Not just some story that he had heard whispered from time to time. It was no longer folklore: it existed, it was tangible. He felt he could reach out and touch it.

He stood and placed the letters on the pile for his great-grandfather: Robert S Perkins. He noticed that the record had finished, so he flipped the disc and lowered the stylus. The second part was just about to begin.

NINETEEN

As far as Ian could tell, there was only one reason that Stuart had become closer to his father: the farm. Ever since the conversation about the curse on Stuart's sixteenth birthday they had become inseparable. Ian had asked Stuart on numerous occasions where they had got to on the evening that they failed to return home until the dead of night, but Stuart never really gave him a proper answer. In fact, Stuart never really gave Ian a proper answer about anything anymore.

Ian often wondered where Stuart and his father had been on the tractor that night, but no-one seemed willing to talk, and Ian quickly gave up. Life continued in the same pattern: the boys returned from school and went out with their father to help on the farm.

On the day that Ian reached his sixteenth birthday, he woke early. He lay and stared at the ceiling, little butterflies exciting him within as he imagined spending time with his father by the stream, his first beer in hand.

As expected, his father was already gone by the time he got downstairs, and it was his mother who greeted him at the kitchen table with bacon sandwiches and gifts before school – records, books and new clothes. Stuart was also absent; now eighteen with school behind him, he was a full-time farmhand. Ian finished his breakfast quickly, eager to get the school day out of the way. Eager to get back home again.

It had worked.

It seemed like no time at all had passed, a simple click of the fingers, and Ian was leaving the village school and making his way back across the fields towards the cottage. He could see the outline of the giant sycamore tree from miles away, each step making it that little bit bigger. The back of his shirt was soaking, his hair dripping. Despite the heat, when he reached the end of the driveway he broke out into a sprint for the last twenty or so metres. He clattered through the front door and threw his school bag on the floor.

Then he was up the stairs, three at a time, and into his bedroom. He peeled off his shirt and trousers and changed into an old T-shirt and shorts. Then, like a hurricane, he was back down the stairs and into the kitchen. He expected to see his mother, but the kitchen was empty. The French windows were already open and he stepped out into the garden. He lifted his hand to shade himself from the sun and his eyes followed the empty washing line down to the bottom of the garden. There was no one there either. He had expected to see his father and brother atop the tractor, waiting for him. He pulled on his farm boots and strolled down the garden. Perhaps they had been held up somewhere.

He got to the stone wall at the end of the garden and stood with his arms outstretched and his hands on top of the wall as if he were holding it to stop it collapsing. He stretched his

147

back and lifted his head, eying the landscape. There was no sight of them. He climbed and stood on top of the wall to get a better view. Aside from the odd bird swooping and diving in the distance, the landscape was entirely still. A living watercolour. He stayed on the wall for around ten minutes, scouting the landscape and hoping that at any moment he'd hear the chug-chug-chug of the tractor coming over the fields in the distance.

He was thirsty now. A few more minutes passed and then he reluctantly climbed down from the wall and idly made his way back to the house. God, it was hot. He went inside and opened the fridge. Cold air rushed out. It felt nice. Unsure what he was after, he ran his fingers across the various items. He pulled a carton of apple juice from the fridge door and took two large gulps. He was glad his mother wasn't around; she wouldn't approve of him drinking directly from the carton.

He placed it back in the fridge and stood in the kitchen, staring out of the window. Still hoping.

"Hello, birthday boy."

The voice came from behind him. He turned and smiled at his mother. Her arms were full of laundry.

"What are you doing?"

"Oh, nothing," he lied. It was hard to hide his disappointment. He saw Mum's eyes dart somewhere over his shoulder and then back to him.

"I thought they'd be back by now," she said. She continued past him and through the kitchen to the utility room. The door closed behind her. Ian turned and looked out of the window again.

A few moments later she returned, the pile of white laundry replaced by a basket of wet reds and blues. She placed the basket on the kitchen table and slipped on her shoes. "I'm sure they won't be long. Come on, give me a hand with these."

It wasn't quite the birthday treat he anticipated, but at least helping Mum would pass the time until they arrived. Ian collected the peg bag from on top of the washing machine and went into the garden. Mum followed behind, carrying the basket of wet clothes.

After hanging out the washing, Ian sat with his back against the exterior wall, staring down the garden. Inside, Mum busily prepared the birthday tea that apparently just the two of them would be eating together. After tea (into which Mum tried and failed to inject some joy by reminiscing over Ian growing up), he spent the evening flipping between the television in the lounge and the view from the kitchen table. Every so often he would hear a mechanical sound in the distance and leap from the sofa to check if it was them. He'd crane his neck at all angles, peering as far as he could see from the bay window in the lounge. He'd momentarily stop moving, wondering if the tractor was just out of sight behind the giant sycamore that seemed to stare angrily at him. Then, when the sound persisted, he would race to the kitchen, throw the doors open and rush onto the grass, to scan the horizon ahead of him. But each time he was alone, but for the company of the washing, puffing and swaying in the gentle breeze.

Later that evening, when he was in the bath, he imagined he heard the tractor finally returning to the cottage. He leapt up, splashing dirty water over the edges in his haste to throw open the window and stare outside. He raced past his mother along the landing, a towel wrapped around his waist, to his bedroom to check the view at the front. He was greeted with the same view of nothing.

As Ian dressed for bed, Mum shouted at him to come downstairs. He was sure that there was something in the way she called his name. An audible enthusiasm. The sun had begun to set at nine fifteen, and half an hour later it had disappeared to the other side of the earth for another day. It was now dark. He made his way down the stairs, following Mum's voice, which repeated his name. All of the lights were off, and as he rounded the wooden post at the bottom of the stairs he heard his name again, coming from the kitchen. This time it sounded more like a whisper. The volume lowered as he got closer.

He walked slowly, and as he did he allowed the thought to cross his mind that perhaps Dad and Stuart had returned. Maybe there was a surprise waiting for him. In the dark. Like the giant surprise parties he had seen on television, where the lead character returns home, disappointed, to what they think is an empty house and it turns out that everyone they have ever met is standing in a giant crescent awaiting them.

Ian followed the voice down the hall. It was a simple whisper, repeating his name. A female, almost infant-like voice. It had to be his mother's. There were no other females in the house.

As he reached the frame of the kitchen door, he spoke for the first time.

"Hello?"

There was no response, and he felt a draught cross the gap between his pyjama top and bottoms. It was only gentle, but enough for the fair hairs on his back to stand on end. He repeated his greeting. The only light came from the red digital clock on the oven to his left. The floor was cold and he stood frozen for a moment. He wondered whether this was a dream.

Then the voice said his name again. He followed it, feeling his way around the work surface until he reached the kitchen table. He clasped his hands around its edges. In the moonlight that trickled in through the closed curtains he was sure he could make out a dark shape sitting at the far end of the table. Maybe. He squinted, urging his eyes to adjust to the darkness. It was impossible to make out anything further; it was almost as if it was *just a feeling* that someone was sitting there, an almost imperceptible shadow slightly obscuring the white wall behind it. He reached for the light switch.

"Don't," the gentle voice said.

His finger remained on the switch, his eyes staring into the darkness.

"Mum?" he said, knowing that it wasn't. The hairs on his arms lifted. His feet were instantly numbed by the cold, and it rose rapidly up his legs and through his body. He began to shake. "Mum?" he said, louder. "Mum?"

He heard a click and the lights above him came on.

"Ian?"

He turned away from the direction of the shape to see his mother's face at the door. She smiled. "Where have you been?"

He paused. "Here."

"We've been waiting for you in the dining room. Come on."

Ian followed his mother into the darkness of the hall and into the dining room. At the table sat his father and brother, almost smiling.

"Happy birthday, son," Dad said. "Sorry, we, er, got held up. Didn't we?"

He nudged Stuart. Stuart nodded. "Yeah."

In the middle of the table was a large, circular cake. It was iced half in blue, half in green. Separating the two was a crudely made red tractor shape. It was driving toward a dark brown tree with huge outreaching branches. Sixteen candles were lit evenly around the perimeter. Ian stood with his mouth open, his face expressionless.

"Don't you like it?" Mum said.

Ian slowly turned and looked at her.

"It's supposed to be the farm," she said, "and there are sixteen candles."

Ian managed a slight smile.

"It's taken me most of the day. It's been a nightmare trying to stop you seeing what I was doing."

"Yeah, it's really good." This was perhaps overstating it, but she had certainly improved over the previous two years.

"Come on then," said Dad. He began to sing the opening

line of 'Happy Birthday' and nudged Stuart again, who joined in instantly. Mum followed. After three cheers, Ian blew the candles out.

"Shall we cut it now?" said Mum.

"Nah," Ian replied. "I'm really tired. Can we have it tomorrow?"

"Of course," said Mum.

"I'm gonna go up."

"Okay."

"G'night, son," said Dad. "Happy birthday."

Ian made his way into the darkness of the hall and to the bottom of the stairs. He paused and listened. Aside from his mother's voice, muffled by the dining room door, he didn't hear another sound as he continued upstairs and to bed.

TWENTY

The next week drifted. Ian spent every waking hour in the study. Aside from the light and dark outside it was impossible to know that time was even passing. Ian was entirely committed to the task before him. Emails and 'work' for the first twenty minutes of the day, no more. The bare minimum. There was no television. No internet. A self-enforced embargo. The world could have been under attack by extra-terrestrials and Ian wouldn't have known. Unless they had chosen to land at the end of the drive.

There were no distractions in the house and Ian chose to treat his time alone as some kind of gift. Although he was a strong atheist, he had a feeling that some unknown presence or force had marked these days on a giant calendar in the sky. They had been circled in red, and it had been decided on his behalf that these days were his – freed up so he could find a solution to this mystery.

The distraction of Rachel and Harry had also been removed. In the case of Rachel, Ian concluded that this was probably a blessing. He couldn't bear her scowling and sulking, which would invariably come when she found out that he was permanently living in the study. Recently, just her very presence in the house had seemed to bring about an atmosphere of sorrow, an unspoken air of misery that seeped into every room. He could feel it when he walked through the hall and up the stairs, an invisible mist that lingered in the rooms she had recently left. If he entered a room and found her there, the heaviness in the air was even more apparent. He could almost taste it. It made her presence close to unbearable. Suffocating.

Harry's absence was less palatable. He was the antidote for Rachel's mist, his innocence and happy demeanour instantly clearing the fog and giving Ian a reason for his existence. On the first day after Rachel left, it was a struggle for Ian to come to terms with Harry's absence. But he soon realised that if this time had been designated for Ian, it was better that Harry was with Rachel. It would give Ian time to focus on the paperwork, without distraction, ensuring that he picked through every detail, every piece of evidence, so the final conclusion would be watertight. Unquestionable.

Each day he woke early, made coffee and did the bare minimum of work. Then he was in the study on his hands and knees, taking each page and reading it, highlighting it, filing it. His only other distraction was breaking every half an hour to flip whatever record was playing. There were numerous albums he had bought over the years on the recommendation of friends or music critics that he had never played, albums that had received great reviews that Ian had purchased without ever hearing a song. There were records by bands that Ian had read about and simply found interesting, and ones he'd bought simply because he liked the name of the band. Music was the only thing that Ian really spent his money on. The gift of free time allowed him to finally listen to the horde of unknown music that surrounded him on the walls above.

He didn't speak to Rachel a single time in those first three days. He decided on the first day that he wasn't going to contact her. She had asked as much in her note. Much as he wanted to speak to her, and especially Harry, he would let her work this through at her own pace. There was, of course, the possibility that his lack of contact would be interpreted as disinterest on his part, but there was nothing he could do about that. He had learned that whatever good intentions he may have, they were always open to interpretation by Rachel. It seemed to him that the closer you were to someone, the more possibility there was that they would interpret something you did or said in a different way than it was intended. Perhaps it was because they knew you the best, knew how you thought, and therefore they looked for hidden agendas based on your previous actions. Anyway, he was prepared to take a chance this time: he'd leave it to Rachel to contact him.

It was the morning of the fourth day that she telephoned him. Ian didn't hear the phone at first, the sound of Wintersleep so loud that he had missed her call three times. It was only when the record finished playing and the phone rang again that he picked it up.

"Are you ignoring me?" she said. It was a bad way to begin the conversation and immediately Ian felt on edge.

"No, not at all."

"Where were you?"

"Just in the study. I've got music on." Quickly, before she could respond, he asked, "How's things?"

"Not bad," she said, softening. "Been sleeping a bit better. In fact, we both have."

"Good. How's your mother?"

"She's okay. You know how she is, always the same."

"Yeah, I do. Give her my love."

"I will."

"So?" Rachel stretched out the word, as if deciding what to attach to the end. And then…nothing.

Ian moved another piece of paper onto the correct pile. There was less than a handful now to sort through.

"So?" he repeated back to her.

"Er, well, I suppose I was just seeing if you were okay?"

"Yeah, not bad," he said. He held the phone between his shoulder and ear so he could get the lid off the highlighter pen. "Busy."

"Right," she said.

He drew the pen across the name 'George Perkins', illuminating it in green.

"Yeah, loads to do."

Her tone changed. "Are you still going through all those papers?"

"Yep," he confirmed. He scanned the next sheet. "Nearly there now."

"What are you hoping to find in all that rubbish, Ian?" she said bluntly.

157

"It's not rubbish. It's history. My history."

"But what does it prove, Ian?"

"Well, I don't know," he said, highlighting the name 'George Perkins' on the page in front of him. "I've not got through it all yet."

"You do know that you're wasting your time."

"We'll see," he said.

"Listen, you're obviously busy so I'm gonna go."

"Okay," he said. He was relieved. Once again, the conversation wasn't going anywhere.

"Bye."

"Yeah, bye."

Ian pressed the red button on the screen. He held the paper with his right hand and drew a straight green line through the name. He filed the sheet and collected the next one. With a bit of luck, he would have sorted all the papers into name order by bedtime tonight.

Rachel put the phone down and pushed her face into the pillow. She hoped that it would drown out the deep, long sobs that came from inside her and made her body physically jolt as she released them. She didn't want her mother to hear her. The door opened.

She felt a hand on her hip, another on her hair. The hand stroked her hair, smoothing it. She continued to sob loudly, each stroke allowing her to release some more of the pain she felt. Her stomach pulled in and then pushed out with each breath. In between her howls, she could hear the soft, calming voice of her mother, soothing her in the same way she would have done when Rachel was a baby.

The scene continued for several minutes, until Rachel's breaths became less heavy and her involuntary movements subsided. She pulled her face from the pillow for the first time since the phone call had ended. Her mother pushed Rachel's hair from her eyes and handed her a tissue.

Her eyes were red. A sprinkling of cracked black mascara surrounded them.

Her mother smiled sympathetically.

"He didn't even mention Harry," Rachel sobbed. She was suddenly angry. "Not once."

TWENTY-ONE

University was always the place where Ian would end up.

Stuart on the farm.

Ian at university.

They were invisible paths drawn (or ploughed, in Stuart's case) for each of them at a young age.

Nobody had ever even talked about it. Well, not in so many words. It was always inference. Inference and expectation. There had never been an open conversation about where Ian would fit into the family plan. He had no idea what the plan was. If it even existed, he had never seen it.

After Stuart's sixteenth birthday, it was always clear that Stuart was to go nowhere. The plan set for him was to farm the land and carry on the family tradition. And as far as Ian could see, Stuart seemed more than happy to do this. He worked hard alongside his father from the moment the sun rose until the moment it fell behind the horizon, seven days a week.

Ian's sixteenth birthday, of course, had not been an occasion for setting future paths. The experience of that night stayed with him and jumped into his thoughts almost daily. Especially during the night. As the years passed, his father (through near silence and non-communication) made it clear that Ian wasn't going to be staying at the farm. And so, he was silently steered into doing something that no other member of the Perkins family had ever done: go to college and then get a degree. The fact that Stuart left school with no qualifications seemed to be of little consequence to his parents. For Ian, it was an altogether different story. Each report sent home from college was carefully scrutinised by Dad, who demanded to know why the eighty per cent test score he had achieved wasn't ninety per cent.

And so, Ian quietly got on with what was expected of him. He achieved high grades simply to avoid tirades, to avoid the furious look on Dad's face. When invariably he did do well, the look of fury was replaced with a begrudging expectant look.

It made Ian sick.

He tried to discuss Dad's attitude with Mum, but she would comment that Dad simply wanted the best for Ian. Her response was no more than Ian expected. He couldn't remember a time she had ever stood up to Dad. Defending the indefensible. She would have said the grass was red if Dad had told her to.

Ian didn't feel that his father wanted the best for him. Dad didn't seem to care. It seemed instead that Stuart was the only one that mattered. It was almost as if Dad was compelled to spend every second with Stuart, as if he knew Stuart's time was finite – that he had turned over an hourglass on the day that Stuart was born and now he could see that the majority of the sand had slipped away.

The accompanying hourglass for Ian remained full.

Blocked where the top narrowed to the bottom.

There was no college in the local village and so Ian had to

travel each day by bus to the nearest town. It didn't matter that his day was nearly three hours longer than his normal school day. He was happy to be away from the cottage. It wasn't the atmosphere there that bothered him. He was used to that; he didn't know anything different. No, it was the isolation of the cottage that got to him.

Each evening as Ian made his way home, he was overcome by a deep feeling of dread that increased in intensity as the bus got ever closer. By the time the bus came to a stop on the main road at the end of the lane, his heart was beating relentlessly. And as he rounded the corner and the enormous sycamore tree came into view, the feeling gripped him entirely, pulling the muscles around his heart tightly. On the dark winter nights, when daylight was shortest, he imagined the shadowy branches forming into a twisted wooden hand and reaching down and pulling his heart directly from his chest. Sometimes – the worst times – when the feeling overwhelmed him, he would race past the tree, refusing to look at it, and fall, almost breathless, through the front door.

The house was usually empty. Latterly, possibly in an attempt to avoid the cottage herself, Mum had taken up a number of classes in the village. Painting was one, swimming another. Dad and Stuart – whatever the weather – would be out somewhere on the land. Working. Together.

If, when empty, the cottage was silent then perhaps being at home alone wouldn't have been so bad. But it wasn't. It was an old building that creaked as the internal wooden structure expanded and contracted each day. On a windy day the attic floor would groan, and as the temperature dropped in the autumn the huge metal bolts that kept the walls upright would screech beneath Ian's bed. He wasn't usually scared in the house. He had lived there all his life and he understood the almost living nature of the property. He understood that some of the rooms seemed to whisper to him as he went past them, that some doors would simply slam shut when they did not wish anyone to enter the room they guarded. The character of the cottage fuelled his imagination and he spent most evenings lying on his bed surrounded by books and journals filled with the stories he wrote. He would note down almost anything that happened in the cottage and turn events into short stories about ghosts and hidden secrets. He spent the rest of his time reading or listening to music. And these were his college years: alone, but for the characters that lived in his mind.

On the morning that Ian finally escaped the cottage, the floor-to-ceiling bookcase at the end of his bed was packed full of his favourite books. Little bits of paper stuck out of the top of them, highlighting sentences that he especially liked or paragraphs that evoked powerful feelings within him.

It was nearly time to go, and he eyed the clothes that were trying to escape from the open suitcase on his bed, wondering if he had forgotten anything. He heard a car horn, and glanced out of the window to see Dad beckoning him to the car. He was tapping his watch. Mum stood alongside him, her face obscured by a thick branch from the tree. Ian quickly retrieved two books filled with Roald Dahl's short stories and threw them on top of his clothes. He zipped the suitcase around three sides and lifted it to the floor.

"We're late," said Dad as Ian struggled through the front door with his case.

"Let's just get a photo," said Mum. Dad tutted.

Ian stopped in front of the cottage door, his suitcase on the ground next to him. Mum suggested that he smile, and he pulled a grin that was somewhere between relief and excitement. It was not dissimilar to the look on the face of an exonerated victim of a miscarriage of justice. It suddenly occurred to Mum that it would be nice to have Stuart in the photograph, and she called him over. He trudged out of the front door and stood next to Ian, who flung an arm around his shoulders and pulled him closer. Stuart sprung back rigidly and the two brothers stood alongside each other, changing their facial expressions until their mother was satisfied.

The car horn sounded. "Can we get going now?" said Dad through the window.

"Yes, of course, dear," said Mum.

"I've got better things to do today than drive for four hours."

Ian hugged his mother and as they parted she held his shoulders for a second and looked into his eyes. "Be safe," she said.

"I will."

Ian turned to Stuart. "So, I'll see you soon."

Stuart nodded and offered his hand. Ian shook it.

"I'll get that," said Stuart, pointing the suitcase. He carried it to the back of the car and lifted it inside.

Ian climbed into the car.

"So..." Dad let out a long sigh. "Are we finally ready?"

Ian closed the car door. "Yep," he said.

As the car reversed out of the drive Ian waved to Mum, who seemed to be crying. The tree's branches reminded Ian of a giant claw, and they waved eerily in unison with his mother, swaying backwards and forwards in perfect synchronicity.

TWENTY-TWO

Ian locked the study door and carefully posted the key into his pocket. He tapped it just to ensure that he could feel it against his thigh. He stretched and yawned. It had been a good day. Everything was now in order, every single document carefully laid out in neat piles, one for each family member.

He was definitely getting closer.

He checked the front door was locked and began his walk up the stairs. He pulled back his shirt sleeve to see his watch: it was ten minutes to midnight; he was ready for bed. As he reached the final few stairs, he noticed that Harry's bedroom door was wide open and the light was on. He couldn't be certain, but he thought that it had been closed that morning. Just like every other morning that week. He popped his head around the door. Everything seemed to be in place. He switched off the light and pulled the door firmly closed.

The bathroom mirror told him he was exhausted. As he brushed his teeth he noticed a gathering of new grey hairs above his ears. He was sure that they hadn't been there the last time he looked. Then again, he couldn't remember the last time he'd looked. Checking his appearance had been pretty low in priority for many months now. Perhaps the grey hairs had been there all along. One thing was for sure: he was looking his age. He spat the toothpaste into the sink and undressed.

The bedroom was unusually cold. He clicked off the light. And shivered.

He climbed into bed and pulled the duvet tightly around him. It would soon warm up. He closed his eyes. His thoughts were swimming with the names of his forefathers. Different names would appear, bouncing in from the edges of his mind, spinning and rotating as he tried to work how each was related to the next. This was not a job for today, for now; the family tree was tomorrow's job. He just wanted to switch off from it, get a good night's sleep and be fresh for the morning. He shuffled his position. The names kept appearing. He needed the night to end. But sleep didn't appear to be arriving anytime soon.

Onto his front.

His side.

Henry Perkins.

His back.

His arm under the pillow.

George Perkins.

Breathe through his mouth.

His arm above the pillow.

Robert Perkins.

Please let me sleep.

Stop.

Turn over.

I'm so, so tired.

Please.

His brain continued to whir, throwing grainy black-and-

167

white images from the documents into his mind.

Turn over.

Breathe through his nose.

Try to blank out his mind.

It worked.

For less than a moment.

Stephen Perkins.

George Perkins.

George Perkins.

Stephen Perkins.

Robert Perkins.

The names accelerated.

Please.

Let.

Me.

Sleep.

And then, almost inevitably, his thoughts turned to the curse.

The dog.

The tree.

That was it.

He angrily unwrapped his arms from inside the duvet and thrust an arm out toward the bedside table. It was so cold. His fingers felt around until they reached the switch for the lamp. He clicked it.

There was a boy. A small boy. He was standing, smiling, inches away from Ian's outstretched hand. Ian pulled his arm away, fed it back under the duvet and grabbed at the fabric to cover his face. The bulb extinguished and the bedroom was dark again.

Ian realised that he was entirely under the duvet except for his right foot. His exposed toes hurt from the cold. He pulled the foot back under the duvet and rubbed it on his opposite calf to warm it. The heavy duvet cocooned him, the fabric following the contours of his face exactly. His breathing was deep and he could faintly smell mint in the enclosed area. His heart raced. His whole body was cold again.

He'd definitely seen him, the boy. He was sure of it. Standing alongside Ian, perfectly still, a fixed smile on his face. And that was all he'd seen. A split-second, a simple instant, and then the boy was gone. Ian could actually feel the shape of his heart distorting as the blood pumped through. He imagined an emergency alarm sounding and all employees being called to the factory floor to do all they could to keep his heart from stopping altogether.

He wasn't sure whether the boy had disappeared with the light or he was still there, standing in the darkness, patiently waiting for Ian to look at him again. Ian concentrated on his breathing; he needed to slow it down or he feared he could have a heart attack right there and then. The duvet was slightly damp where his mouth was. His deep breaths slowed to little, rapid intakes, the sound of a bicycle tyre being inflated by a hand pump.

He knew he couldn't continue to hide under the covers; it

was too claustrophobic and the sound of his own breathing was making him more anxious. Every hair on his body stood up, pushed higher by goose pimples desperately trying to catch some warmth. There was none. It was so cold. He needed to get out of there. He pushed the same arm out of the duvet, half-expecting it to touch the little boy. He reached around again for the switch. He clicked it and pulled his arm back under the duvet, leaving a small gap where the bulb shone through.

He waited for a few moments and then quickly pulled the duvet away from his face and stared straight at the ceiling. Slowly, he turned his head to the side, to where the boy had been. He was gone. Ian pulled himself into a sitting position, his back against the headboard, and scanned the rest of the room. It was empty. Warm air began to surround him and he rubbed both arms with his hands.

For the next few minutes he sat and watched nothing unfold in front of him. He questioned whether the event had even taken place. He checked the time. It was now after two. He needed sleep. His brain obviously hadn't been informed. It was still wide awake. He picked up a book from the bedside table and read until the sentences began to repeat and his vision became blurred. He dropped the book onto the floor next to him and rested his head on the pillow.

His sleep was filled with dreams of the boy. In his nightmare, the boy lay next to him, where Rachel used to be. Facing him. Smiling. Ian had his arm around the boy, stroking his hair, coaxing him to sleep. The boy would begin to drift, his eyes closing as sleep enveloped him. For a few moments the room would be silent. And then, as Ian watched, the boy would begin screaming. His face would turn red. Blotchy. And he would be shouting, screeching. The words were indecipherable. The volume was unbearable. It was all Ian could do to hold him and comfort him. The boy would become calm and his face would be restful again. A picture of peace. And then the cycle would repeat and the noise would begin again. The shouting. The silence. Over and over.

And then, as the sun began to rise for a new day, the little boy suddenly appeared above Ian and fell from the ceiling, screaming. His body landed on Ian's face, covering his nose and mouth. Ian couldn't move. The boy was a dead weight. He was trapped and slowly suffocating, disappearing into the darkness.

That was when Ian woke.

It was five thirty in the morning.

It was time to get up.

TWENTY-THREE

Ian only returned to the cottage five times throughout his entire three years at university. Most of the friends he made would escape back to the comfort of their home life at any opportunity – home, where meals were cooked and dirty clothes miraculously washed and ironed within a day or two.

It was different for Ian. In his first year he had returned at Christmas time. His father had collected him, and the two-hour drive was enough for them to say everything that they needed to one another. The words they shared for the remainder of the holiday were few and awkward.

On Ian's first night home in more than three months, his mother prepared a special meal. The two of them sat down together in the dining room to eat it. Mum set the table neatly and lit candles down the centre of the table. She placed his plate down in front of Ian. Almost half the plate was filled with a huge piece of pastry. Beneath it were potatoes and venison. The pie stood at least three inches from the plate. The other half of the plate was stacked to an equal height with broccoli and mashed potato. Mum informed him it was his favourite. Ian didn't want to spoil the occasion and chose not to correct her.

She patted his hand and returned to the kitchen. Moments later she returned with her own plate, which she placed on the table.

"Where's your pie?" Ian asked, noticing that his mother's meal consisted of four pieces of broccoli.

"Oh, mine's in the bin," she said gently to him.

"Why?" he asked.

"I don't like pie," she said. She didn't look at him. Instead she seemed to be speaking to somebody behind him. "But you already know that."

Ian pushed a forkful of mash into his mouth and chewed slowly.

"Anyway, enough about food," Mum said. "Let's find out how my boy is enjoying big school."

After Christmas, Ian made an excuse about returning to university early, some story about having an assignment to finish. Dad seemed more than happy to get him back and was unusually chatty on the return journey.

After that, Ian stayed away whenever he possibly could, spending holidays with friends or working in a small record shop in the university town. He only went back to the cottage when absolutely necessary. Toward the end of his final year, an absolutely necessary time occurred. Stuart was getting married.

The whole thing had come completely out of the blue. It was true that Ian rarely spoke to his brother. In fact, he rarely spoke to any of the family. He did make a point of telephoning home every couple of weeks, but the conversations were usually short.

He'd begun to doubt whether his mother even knew where he was or what he was doing. The conversation would consist of the same questions each time, his answers met by an empty silence as if Mum hadn't listened to or understood his response. Then she'd move on to the next question. When the questions were exhausted she would end the call. On occasion, Ian would hear his brother's gruff voice at the end of the telephone and they'd share the barest of greetings before the phone was passed to Mum.

Still, when Ian received an invitation through the post, inviting him to the marriage of Stuart Perkins and Gillian Harrison, he immediately telephoned home to congratulate his brother. He hadn't even known that Stuart had a girlfriend, never mind one that he was about to marry. It took three days to eventually speak to somebody at the cottage. Mum explained that she had been out swimming and painting for the last few days.

"Is Stuart there?" Ian asked.

"Who?"

"Stuart?"

"Er, oh no. He's not. He'll be on a tractor." She giggled; her voice sounded almost childlike.

"Right. Mum? Why didn't you tell me Stuart was getting married?"

"Didn't I?" she asked.

"No. You didn't."

"Oh dear, silly me. Well, they have to do it pretty quickly, you know."

"Why?"

"Your daddy insisted."

Ian stared into the telephone. Daddy?

"Why?"

"Because of the little boy."

"Pardon?"

"The little boy. He's coming soon!" She sang the last three words.

"What do you mean?"

"Stuart and Gillian's baby boy."

Ian relaxed.

So, Gillian –whoever the hell she was – was pregnant.

Thank God.

TWENTY-FOUR

Ian unlocked the study door. He didn't care that it was before
six. He was just glad to be away from his bedroom. As he waited
for the computer to start, he tried to make sense of the events
of the previous night. In hindsight, he wasn't sure whether the
whole thing had been a dream. That would make sense. The
little boy screaming and falling had definitely been a dream,
he knew that much. But the same boy standing by his bed had
seemed far more real. Ian was sure that he wasn't even asleep
then.

He logged on to his emails and began scrolling through and
deleting them, the same as every other day this week. There
was one email accompanied by a small red exclamation mark.
The subject line read simply 'URGENT'. Ian clicked and read
the text on the screen. It was from his boss. Or (soon-to-be) ex-
boss. The email informed him that he had been 'relieved of his
editorial duties' with 'immediate effect'. The reason was simple:
several of the website's sponsors had threatened to terminate
their contracts with the site because they didn't want to be
'associated with the blasphemous, racist, profanity-laden and
wholly inappropriate content that the current editor supports'.
Beneath there was a link to the article they were referring to,
and a note that it had now been removed from the site.

Ian clicked the link and read for the first time the article he had approved a few days earlier. It was a review of a new film. Well, it was supposed to be. Instead, the contributor had used the forum to attack the lead character – her upbringing, background and beliefs. In addition, he had chosen to liken her to his (now) ex-girlfriend. Ian's heart sank. His boss was correct. There was no question that approving the article was a sackable offence. If Ian had been in the same position, he too would have sacked the editor. Publishing the article was totally indefensible.

Ian sat for a moment, and then began to reply. But it was pointless. There was nothing to say. *Anyway*, he thought, *it'll have to wait*. There was much more serious work to be getting on with.

Ian began by removing carefully labelled piles of paper from the desk. He lifted each one by one and placed them on the floor behind his chair. He needed the space. Once the desk was clear, he went over to the printer and collected a handful of blank sheets of paper.

Starting in the top left-hand corner, he laid them out, perfectly tessellated across the desk, the edges of each sheet touching the one to its right and the one below. Using tape, he carefully fixed them together until he had one enormous sheet. He lifted it and turned it over.

He was ready.

Toward the very bottom he drew a rectangle, and inside it he entered his own name and date of birth. Alongside it he did the same for Rachel, and he drew a line connecting the two boxes. Beneath that he drew two lines that connected to a box containing Harry's name.

He continued his work, drawing boxes and neatly writing the names of his immediate family: his parents, his brother, Uncle Stephen. Once he had exhausted the names he could immediately bring to mind, he began to make his way through the piles of paper that surrounded him in every direction. He selected the pile nearest to him and pored through the contents, trying to make a connection between that individual and the people already drawn on the sheet.

In some cases it was easy: a person was directly referenced in an old newspaper clipping or obituary, their date of death and the names of their surviving family members noted. When Ian was sure of a connection, he would draw another box on the giant sheet and insert the name of the relative into the family tree. It was like a giant jigsaw puzzle, each relative fitting together with another.

The difficulty was the sheer number of people. The Perkins family seemed never-ending. Finding the relationships between some of the individuals was near-impossible. Some shared the same Christian name. Others were known by their middle names. Others married and changed names. He would only add a new box to the family tree when he was absolutely sure. Or so he thought.

As he moved around the piles of paperwork, he soon discovered that he had made an error – that one individual wasn't actually another's husband; they were brother and sister. He scribbled out his error. Then he realised that the incorrect assumption of their relationship affected everything. Their children weren't their children, they were nephews and nieces. And so, like a row of dominoes, one simple misjudgement led to everything falling.

It didn't take long for the vast sheet of paper to become a complete mess. Names all over the place. Relationships wrong. He screwed it up and began the process again. And again. And again. He would not be defeated. He would get to the bottom of this mystery and he would prove that the curse did exist.

He would prove it to Rachel.

And once he had, they would be able to move on with their lives.

Move forwards to get back to where they'd once been.

TWENTY-FIVE

Ian found it very strange to see his father smiling. It was uncomfortable. But there Dad was, standing alongside him, beaming.

At the very front of the registry office stood Stuart and Gillian. Ian hadn't seen Stuart look so smart since Uncle Stephen's funeral, and that seemed like a long time ago. In fact, it was a long time ago, more than a quarter of his life. Stuart and Gillian held hands, staring into each other's eyes, repeating the words that the plump lady in the navy suit was saying. They certainly appeared happy enough.

Ian was disappointed that he was meeting his brother's wife – his sister-in-law – for the first time that day. They hadn't even been introduced yet. But, as Gillian's wedding dress confirmed, there hadn't been much time to arrange everything. It looked like the baby could make a surprise appearance at its parents' own wedding. Ian looked around. There were no more than thirty people in the room. He didn't recognise any of them – aside from his own parents, of course.

After the wedding, the guests were invited to the local village hall for the reception. This was typical of Stuart. There were plenty of nice hotels within twenty miles, but he'd chosen the village hall to make a statement: that if there was a world outside the village, Stuart was never going to visit it. He was born here and he was going to die here.

Ian entered the hall alone.

The local Scouts met here on Tuesdays, and there were coffee mornings on Wednesdays and Fridays. There was a knitting club, a watercolour group and a Bible class, that kind of thing. The wooden floor had seen thousands of feet since it was laid forty years earlier. On each side of the room were huge glass windows, small strips of wall separating them. At one end of the hall was a stage. At the other end, by the entrance, was a small kitchen. In it was a giant tea urn that was always hot.

Today, several tables had been arranged as three sides of a square. The bride and groom sat at the table that joined the other two edges. They were flanked by their parents. The other guests sat on either side of the square. Ian's name card was positioned right at the very end, as far away from the bride and groom as he could be. Directly ahead of them was the stage, and Ian wondered whether somebody might get up and perform later. As long as it wasn't him, he was happy.

Over the course of the meal, Ian realised that the other guests were not particular welcoming. In fact, that was an understatement: they were distinctly unwelcoming. Aside from making a few attempts at conversation right at the very beginning, Ian ate his three courses in complete silence.

Around him, the guests laughed and joked. From time to time a huge guffaw would echo around the room, each time making Ian jump slightly – a joke that everyone but Ian shared. He noticed his father was smiling. He seemed to be enjoying the day. The two families appeared close.

Ian tried to make eye contact with other guests, but invariably they looked away or pretended not to have seen him. Only his mother returned his smile. He was relieved when his dessert bowl was finally taken away and the waitress brought him a glass of champagne. Gillian's father stood and tapped a glass with his fork. *Thank God*, Ian thought, *it's nearly over*. And at least he'd be party to these jokes.

It was late afternoon when the meal finally ended. The staff began to clear the tables away in preparation for the evening party, which would begin a few hours later. This was Ian's opportunity to finally meet Gillian. It appeared, though, that Stuart had a different idea. He seemed to be doing all he could to deliberately keep them apart. On three separate occasions Ian approached the couple and patiently waited in the background whilst they finished their conversation. Ian would nod or give a little wave just to ensure that Stuart had noticed him standing there. Alone. Awkward. But each time, just as it seemed their conversation was ending and it was Ian's turn, Stuart would make an excuse and quickly shepherd his bride away.

Eventually, Ian gave up. He decided that the only way to get through the day was to become acquainted with the makeshift bar that the staff had built in the corner near the kitchen. In truth, the bar was nothing more than an L-shape formed by pushing a couple of wallpapering tables together. Its legs were buckling under the weight of the cans of cider and bitter. Ian found a seat just within reach of the table and took a can. As the two families lingered outside, having their photographs taken, and the staff worked to decorate the room, Ian helped to relieve the weight from the stricken bar.

Five cans later, the room began to fill.

Ian recognised various faces from the past: Stuart's old school friends, local shopkeepers, teachers, the vicar, farmers and farmworkers. It seemed that the whole village was there. Ian was glad of it. At least there were people who would speak with him. He was hoping someone could tell him at least a few basic facts about his new sister-in-law. He was embarrassed that he knew nothing about her or her family. He didn't know her age. Where she was from. Nothing. Leading up to the wedding he had tried to question his mother, but this was close to useless. Mostly now she couldn't even remember *his* name. He hadn't even tried speaking to his father. Nor Stuart.

As the evening went on, Ian managed to obtain small scraps of information about Gillian from other guests. He gleaned that Gillian was two years younger than Stuart and that her father was also a farmer. Gillian and her family owned a farm about ten miles away from the cottage. Not the next village, but the one after that. Their farm had been in the family for hundreds of years, apparently. She and Stuart had met at a ceilidh held locally to celebrate the end of the harvest. It was there, in a car outside, that they had drunkenly chosen to get to know one another better. And today, the wedding, was the result of that.

Numerous times during the evening Ian considered leaving the wedding party and going back to the cottage. But he felt he owed it to his brother to stay until the end. He wasn't sure why. As it got to eleven, though, and the alcohol began to take hold, he'd had enough. He was leaving the party and the village, for good. He had no intention of ever coming back. Nobody would miss him. He no longer cared that he hadn't managed to speak with Gillian. Fuck her. Fuck them all. Unsteadily, he got to his feet, took a breath, and made his way out of the village hall and onto the small lawn outside.

It was lighter outside than inside the hall. Small pockets of smokers were there, laughing and drinking, glad to escape the damp heat of the party. Ian glanced around, ensuring that he didn't know any of the people gathered. The last thing he wanted was some old school friend shouting his name and drawing attention to him as he made his escape. When he was sure that he was safe, he staggered away from the hall toward the cover of a large brightly lit tree halfway between the party and the freedom of the thin, winding road beyond. There was a stile a few hundred yards up the road; a quick hop over that and he'd be onto the fields. Then it was only forty-five minutes along the path, past where Uncle Stephen had died, to home.

The return to the village was suffocating him. The people, their attitudes, their opinions...it was all so claustrophobic. It was evident that he didn't fit in around here. Perhaps he never really had. He couldn't work out whether things had changed or the feeling of suffocation came from the fact that they hadn't. Aside from seeing his mother (who, as far as he could tell, was losing touch with reality altogether), there seemed to be little point in visiting at all anymore. The people who had remained in the village were likely to stay the same forever. Of course they'd get older, but mentally they'd remain the same: scared of change, scared of what was over the other side of the hill, their development crippled by stories of how their forefathers had lived and therefore how they must live.

Ian wasn't going to fall into the same trap. Indeed, even if he had wanted to stay, it seemed he had already been rejected by the village. Three years earlier he had actually dared to leave, and at the very moment he did the village had spat him out and pulled up the drawbridge.

You dare to leave this place.

You're out.

Permanently.

A circular green bench followed the circumference of the thick trunk of the tree. Fairy lights hung in the branches above, flickering in the darkness of the leaves like tiny stars. Ian took one last glance back at the village hall and sure that no-one had seen his exit, he moved around to the other side of the tree and out of view. He threw himself down on the seat and panted, his head in his hands, facing the ground. He was slightly dizzy now and the short dash had made him feel a little sick. He decided to take a quick rest and then make a final run toward the low stone wall that surrounded the gardens. A quick hop over it, and in a hundred yards or so he'd be completely out of sight.

As he lifted his head, he was taken completely by surprise:

his father was already sitting on the bench. Dad couldn't have helped but notice Ian arrive, but he didn't turn to face him. He just stared into the night sky, his thoughts very much elsewhere. Ian looked at him, wondering whether he should speak and break the apparent trance. Dad looked old. His neatly brushed hair was now messy and lay on top of his head like a pile of sticks. Deep creases ran almost from ear to ear across his forehead, reminding Ian of the ploughed fields behind the cottage. His cheeks and nose were red and ruddy with an explosion of tiny blood vessels. It was the first time in years that Ian had been close enough to his father to notice the change in him. His mouth was slightly open, his breathing shallow, a repeated puff in-out-in-out-in-out-in-out like a miniature steam engine.

Now, Ian wasn't so sure that Dad had even noticed his arrival. He turned and followed his father's line of vision, trying to make out what it was that was capturing his attention. Behind the tall steeple of the church were the golden fields that Ian was about to cross to get home. From here he couldn't see the raised track through the fields or the cottage, but that was the general direction in which his father was staring.

Ian wasn't sure what to do next. He considered gently extracting himself from the situation without speaking. Quietly getting to his feet and continuing to the edge of the grass, over the wall and out of sight. Perhaps Dad wouldn't even know he'd been there. Or maybe Dad didn't care. Maybe he was purposely ignoring Ian. Whatever the reason, Ian was stuck with two choices.

To speak.

Or to leave.

Behind him, on the other side of the tree, somebody dropped a glass, which shattered on the tarmac. It was followed by a loud cheer, then laughter. The smokers' voices lowered to an inaudible gaggle, and Ian was left with the silence beneath the tree. It was time to leave. He couldn't think of anything at all to say to his father. Nothing. Whatever came out of his mouth would sound either forced or disingenuous. He would leave. Now.

Another moment passed. Less than a second. The silence became heavier. Ian put his hands on the bench, ready to lever himself up. He pushed, lifting no more than an inch before he felt his father's hand on his right thigh. Ian glanced down. Dad's hand was enormous, almost covering his thigh completely. Thick black hairs grew like weeds, covering the coarse skin that ran to the ends of his fingers, permanently blackened by fifty years of hard work. The hand pushed down gently, yet firmly enough to help Ian back into his seat. Dad then clasped his hands together and returned them to his lap. His stare remained constant, unwavering.

And then there was silence again.

Ian rested his head back against the sharp trunk of the tree. He stared up the middle of the tree, trying to follow the branches to where they were finally freed by the sky. He contemplated what to do next. There was nothing else for it, it was time to go. If Dad tried to stop him, he would push him away and leave. His father didn't control him anymore. He wasn't tied to this place. The anger grew inside him. The time had come to leave this place of secrets, and family disputes, and whispered conversations, and being shunned. He must disregard the past and accept the fact that these people weren't his family, this place wasn't his home. He must leave everything behind.

But there were so many questions that Ian needed answering before he left. This could be his last and perhaps only chance. He couldn't just walk away without at least asking. If he didn't get an answer, well so be it. At least he would have tried. He ordered the questions in his mind, steeling himself for the fight that was about to take place. He wanted to know why he was treated the way he was. Why his so-called family had ignored his sixteenth birthday. He'd had many years to contemplate this. Things had changed the moment that Uncle Stephen had left. At that exact moment, when Dad had appeared with his gun and sent them all inside. Ian wanted to know what had happened that day, why the whole family had become so fractured. What did Stuart know that Ian didn't? Why had Dad turned Mum into the woman she now was? What had Ian done so wrong to make Dad treat him the way that he did? What was this fucking curse that everyone seemed so preoccupied with?

Ian was ready.

He was leaving.

And it was time to get all of this out. These questions had tortured him for long enough. Just hearing himself say them to his father would be enough of a release.

He put his hands into position and pushed himself up, expecting Dad's hand to reach across for a second time. It didn't. Ian kept moving and a moment later he was on his feet. He looked at Dad, who continued his long stare into the distance. Ian momentarily froze, waiting for Dad to move or speak or do something. Anything would do, anything so Ian could empty his mind.

There wasn't even a flicker.

Nothing.

Ian felt his chest tighten. He wanted this out. It was something he'd carried with him for too long. He urged himself to open his mouth to speak. Just force the first word out. Instead though, he felt tears welling in his eyes and his throat was blocked. He just wanted his father to react in some way – whatever way – and then he could begin and end it all now. He opened his mouth to speak. Instead, he heard a giggle and footsteps shuffling along the path on the other side of the tree. He turned and arched his neck to see.

Stuart and Gillian.

In her heavily pregnant state, Gillian was doing an excellent job of keeping Stuart upright. His shirt was untucked and his tie and jacket were missing. His grey waistcoat sat uncomfortably across his belly, two of the three buttons managing to find the wrong holes. He was smiling and telling Gillian something that she seemed to find funny. Cider sloshed from his can as they got closer.

Ian smiled.

Gillian returned a half-smile and looked at Stuart for further instructions. It took Stuart a moment to see Ian, and when he did his smile disappeared. Gillian looked at the ground.

"Y'seen Dad?" Stuart slurred.

Was that it? The first time Ian had met his brother's wife and this was it? Ian felt his anger rise again; he had just as much to say to Stuart as he did to his father. He stared at Stuart for a moment. He looked exactly the same as Dad, just a younger version. The thick wrinkles were beginning. His hands were already darkened by the tractor oil and the dirt from the land. And then Ian realised exactly what it was that connected Stuart and Dad. It was the weight, the weight of whatever it was that they both carried, the invisible pressure pushing down on them each and every day. In the fields. In the cottage. In bed. In their dreams. In their nightmares.

Ian quickly decided that today wasn't the day for this. Not on Stuart's wedding day. Some other time.

Ian nodded to where Dad was sitting.

Stuart raised his eyebrows and he and Gillian walked around the tree. Ian watched as Stuart stopped in front of their father.

"Dad, you coming inside?"

There was no response. Stuart screwed up his face. He looked puzzled.

"Dad?"

Stuart unclasped himself from Gillian and bent to Dad's eye

level. Off balance, he broke his fall by grabbing at Dad's knees. Gillian laughed. Ian shook his head.

"Dad? What are you looking at? Dad? What are you staring at?"

Ian had seen enough.

It really was time to go.

"I'm off," he said, backing away. "Er, congratulations. Nice to meet you Gillian."

She smiled.

He quickly made his way to the stone wall and climbed over. It was only when he was on the gravel road on the other side, that he turned around. Stuart was between Dad's legs, his head resting on Dad's thigh, his face looking up. Dad had stopped staring now, and his gaze was on Stuart. His giant hand ran up and down Stuart's hair and neck.

He seemed to be crying.

Just as he would be the next time they all met.

TWENTY-SIX

Ian made his way through the kitchen to the French windows yet again. He pulled down hard on the handle, ensuring that it wouldn't move. It was locked. Definitely. He had already done this twice before, but he had to be sure. He couldn't afford his sleep to be interrupted again. Yes, it was certainly locked. As were all the other external doors downstairs. And the study door.

As he passed the study he tried the handle again, just to make sure. Yes, locked. He switched off the light in the hall and began to climb the stairs. It had been the most successful day so far. He was sure that he had managed to pull together a family tree that went back at least one hundred and fifty years. After several unsuccessful attempts sketching out the names on paper (which quickly became huge screwed-up balls), he had found some software online and carefully tapped in the names and relationships of his ancestors. Six generations of the Perkins family.

As he reached the top of the stairs, he wondered whether he had saved his work. He hadn't yet printed it – he needed to do a little more research before he could consider it a final version. But he must have saved it. Surely. Maybe not. He reached the landing carpet, and immediately spun and made his way back downstairs. He switched on the light and took the key from his pyjama pocket. He was beginning to panic now. He fumbled with the key in the lock and then clicked the door open. The study was dimly lit by the black computer screen and when he hit the keyboard he was relieved to see that the family tree was still on the screen. Just as he had left it.

He clicked the screen and clarified that he had indeed saved his work. He smiled, but just for safety he decided to email himself a copy. He had come so far, he couldn't afford to lose his work now. He was about to leave when he realised that should his computer crash – or, worse still, die overnight – he would not be able to continue his research. Pleased for once with his clarity of thought, he clicked the little printer icon on the screen. The printer rollers began to whir.

He watched until the paper pulled through. As soon as the printer stopped, he grabbed the sheet and held it up in front of him, but it was too dark in the study to read it. As he leaned over the desk to switch off the computer, something passed in front of the window outside. He stopped dead, his back arched over the desk, his right hand on the mouse. Slowly he mustered the courage to raise his head and stare up at the window above him. It was impossible to know what the movement had been, especially through the closed blinds. It was more of a shadow. There was almost no light in the room, but there had certainly been something outside. In the bottom corner of the window. He stood upright and reached for the cord that drew the grey fabric blind upward. His hands trembled, and he willed himself to pull the string.

And then it appeared again. In the exact same place. A dark shadow, the form of a person perhaps. Moving slightly. Ian's heart pounded. If there was somebody outside, he and whoever it was were only a few feet apart. Close enough that if there were no window between them, they could have reached out and shaken hands. Ian squeezed the cord tightly, urging himself to lift the blind. To come face to face with the greyness outside.

He let go, and edged back towards the door, stumbling over the piles of paper that covered the study floor. The shadow seemed to watch him, unmoving. He reached the light switch. The room lit up. Then he took a deep breath, strode back across the room and pulled the cord. The darkness outside spilled into the room as the fabric passed his face. And he stared directly into the eyes of the shadow.

The shadow that was no longer there.

He arched his neck, trying to see around the corner. Just in case whoever it was had been startled by the light and hidden out of view. Aside from the branches of the enormous tree that flashed grey and brown in the wind, there was nothing. Puzzled, he pulled the blind back down. The shadow reappeared, edging into view from the same position. He yanked the blind up quickly, trying to catch out the shadow before it disappeared again. As he did, the blind came clattering down from its fixing, stinging Ian's face before coming to rest diagonally across the desk and computer monitor.

Ian put his hand to his head and then looked at his fingers.

There was blood. He held his pyjama sleeve against his forehead and eyed the window.

There was no sign of the shadow.

Ian climbed into bed and turned off his lamp. His head was sore. The cut was a couple of inches long. It wasn't particularly deep, but the area around it had swollen instantly, making it look much worse than it was. To stop the bleeding he had plugged the wound with toilet paper, which was now acting as an adhesive, held in place with two plasters. He adjusted his position to avoid putting any pressure on the wound and closed his eyes.

Immediately, a mental checklist appeared in his mind. Happily, he ticked off each item, satisfied that the house was as secure as could be. He was also pleased that he'd had the foresight to bring the copy of the family tree up to bed with him. It was safely stowed in his bedside drawer. As he waited for sleep to take him, thoughts of the shadow resurged. The need to tend to his head had been a slight distraction, but now that he was alone in the dark he thought about it once more. There had certainly been something there. What, he didn't know. But he was tired. So, so tired. And his head hurt. And for now, at least, he was happy to conclude that the shadow had been exactly that: a shadow. What had cast the shadow, however, he was less clear about.

It was then that he felt a light coldness on his left leg. He kicked out his legs, trying to straighten the duvet to ensure that there were no gaps where air could get in. When he was sure that the duvet was wrapped firmly under his feet, he pulled it up around his neck. Finally, he began to drift off.

His body jolted as he fell deeper and deeper into sleep. At the same time, he felt a slight pulling sensation from around his feet. The tiniest of tugs, like a thumb and forefinger gently trying to remove a thin wooden brick so the tower doesn't collapse. And there it was again, delicately trying to remove the duvet from under his feet. His fall into sleep was temporarily delayed and he lay still, concentrating on what was happening. There were no sounds, just the slight pulling.

And then he felt the cold air come in, winding its way from the outside around his toes. He felt the tugging again. The fabric slipped from beneath his feet. Then his feet were cold, next his ankles. The gap between the bed and the duvet widened further, allowing in more and more icy air. It travelled up his legs. He pulled the duvet up to cover his head, exposing his knees, trying to keep the upper half of his body warm. He wanted to recapture the duvet with his feet, but he couldn't move. He didn't feel trapped, or even frightened, but movement seemed like too much of an effort. The cold continued to find a way in, and it snaked up his body, across his chest, to his upper arms. He knew he should rub himself to get warm but his hands were fixed tightly, grasping the inside of duvet, holding it above his head. He couldn't move them either.

He began to shiver. His mind was now fixated on the coldness transferring through his skin, into him. His teeth began to chatter, and for a moment the clicking sound was all he could hear. The duvet felt like a blanket of ice, so cold it almost felt hot. He could feel the coldness running deep beneath his skin, little tributaries of near-frozen water running endlessly. His face felt numb. The cut on his forehead throbbed.

And then, he was suddenly compelled to lift the duvet. He pulled it away from his face slightly, and from beneath the darkness of the duvet he looked down his naked body to the end of the bed. And there, in the gap where his cocoon met the outside air, was the little boy's face. It was hard to make out in the darkness. But he was smiling.

"Hello," whispered the boy.

TWENTY-SEVEN

Ian hadn't seen any of his family since Stuart's wedding. And now, here they were, thrown together once again like a pile of odd socks.

The day after the wedding, as the train pulled him ever closer to university and ever further away from his family, he'd contemplated the previous evening. The alcohol had worn off and with it the majority of the anger and boldness. He was glad that he and his father hadn't come to blows. It wasn't Ian's style, and in hindsight it would have only made him feel worse. Aggression was part of the Perkins way. Success was achieved by overpowering the weak, bullying them into the submission. Ian had spent the majority of his life breaking that mould. He was quietly pleased that he wasn't one of them. His feelings hadn't changed, of course, he doubted they ever would, but sadly the opportunity to express them had all but disappeared.

And since that time, nearly twelve months before, Ian hadn't returned to Cobweb Cottage. Not once. He remained resolute that he was permanently extracting himself from the family. There was nothing there for him anymore. The only link was his mother, but it was clear from their monthly telephone conversations that her condition had continued to deteriorate. Their conversations had become entirely one-sided, and Ian got the impression that she wasn't even sure to whom she was speaking. It seemed that she needed some kind of medical help, but nobody at the cottage seemed to either notice or care. When he'd asked her directly how she was he'd received an answer completely unrelated to his question. It was less than likely that Mum would ever recognise him properly again.

And it was no coincidence that over the course of the last year, the less Ian had to do with his family, the more his own life had improved. He had met Rachel. He had met her mother, her sister, her wider family. They were the kind of family that he would have liked. He was happy to adopt this one for himself; and if it meant trading his own for them – well, that was all the better.

And now, as the train rumbled back through the familiar countryside toward the village, he wondered what reception he would receive. Nobody had tried to contact him. How could he have been expected to attend the christening if he hadn't known about it? He didn't blame his mother, of course. She simply wasn't capable anymore. As he saw the train's reflection rush by in the lake that ran alongside the tracks, he wondered whether he had actually extracted himself from the family or in actuality he had been excommunicated by them. He didn't suppose it mattered really.

He wished that he had accepted Rachel's offer to accompany him. At least he would have had somebody there to support him. And she had been pestering him for a number of months to meet his family. The picture he had painted had not been favourable. But she was "sure that they were not as bad as he made out". She shouldn't have been. He imagined that when he arrived, nobody would even acknowledge his existence. He'd be yet another family ghost. Invisible and unnecessary. This was the reason he'd decided to book a return ticket for the same day. He would be there for no longer than two hours, and he'd then retreat on the 3.40 p.m. back to Happiness, calling at Acceptance and Appreciation en route.

That fact was, Ian hadn't even intended to make the journey at all. He had only found out about it on social media, and had toyed with the idea of pretending he hadn't for the best part of the week. In need of a second opinion, he had mentioned it to Rachel, and she had informed him that he'd never forgive himself if he didn't attend. He had believed her, and eventually guilt had got the better of him.

The church was full. Overfull. Mourners lined the walls, standing two deep. People were squeezed into the pews, elbows and knees unavoidably touching the ones adjacent. Ian managed to find a place right in the very back corner, standing beneath a large black speaker that was mounted on the wall. He hoped that he wouldn't be noticed here. He looked around the congregation and recognised several people from the wedding. Right at the front, he could see his brother and Gillian. Alongside them was his father and Gillian's parents. He couldn't see his mother.

And then the music started, and from behind him came the tiny pink casket that held the body of the niece that he'd never

200

met.

Over the course of the next hour, the entire shape of the congregation changed. People, once strong and upright, became twisted and crippled, sobbing, holding one another just to stay on their feet. Some couldn't take the weight and collapsed onto their seats. It was the scene after a bomb had exploded. A blitz of grief. Ian stood and watched, his arms folded, a lump in his throat.

The sun illuminated the darkness of the mood. The beauty of the day somehow made the loss greater. Ian waited near the church gates after the funeral, sporadically nodding as people made eye contact as they left. He was compelled to stay until he had been able to offer his condolences directly to Stuart and Gillian. Then he would definitely leave this all behind. He had made that promise to himself before, but this time he meant it. This was it.

People came together and then broke apart, comforting one another, holding one another, offering support. An old school teacher approached him, and Ian excused himself from the group he was with. They shook hands and the teacher offered the family his condolences. It took Ian a moment to realise that the man was referring to his family. In Ian's mind, the funeral for his departure from the family had already taken place. He needed to get away. And soon.

It was now Stuart's turn to hold up Gillian. As they came down the steps from the front of the church, it was clear that she couldn't walk. Stuart wrapped his broad arm around her shoulders and steadied her along the path. She looked tiny. The small groups dotted about the graveyard watched as she collapsed to her knees on the path. And then she was on the ground in a foetal position, howling, her screams muted by her hands, which covered her face. Ian watched from a distance as people crowded around her. One lady knelt and wafted her face with a cardigan. Stuart stood above her, his arms spread out like security at a rock concert, pushing people and shouting at them to stand back, to give her some space.

As Stuart crouched over Gillian, somebody approached and offered a bottle of water. A few minutes later Stuart had managed to get her into a sitting position. Her cheeks were blackened by mascara, her tights ripped and her knees bleeding. Eventually, Stuart helped her to her feet and they began to move slowly down the path in Ian's direction. She was surrounded by family, protected from all sides. As the huddle reached Ian, he stepped forward.

"I just want to say how –"

A large man, his shaved head spattered by numerous scars, stepped across his path. Ian vaguely recognised him from the wedding.

"Move," he said.

Ian let them pass him by. Stuart turned toward Ian just before he disappeared behind the stone church wall and out of sight. Their eyes made contact for the briefest of moments, not enough time for them to do any more than see one another. Neither of their expressions changed. And then Stuart was gone.

Ian sat down on the grass and pulled up his shirt sleeve. Twenty past. He would need to leave for the station in the next half an hour. He posted his finger inside his tie and loosened it. It was hot. Aside from those below the ground, the graveyard was now as good as empty. In the entrance of the church, an old lady stood in the doorway, talking to the vicar. He was holding her hand and seemed to be consoling her. Something told Ian that he knew the lady, but that something didn't tell him where from.

He watched for a few moments, until the lady and the vicar embraced. The vicar helped her down the steps and onto the path outside. From inside the church came a taller man, thin and wiry. Grey tufts of hair, like giant ice cream scoops, sat above his ears. As he stepped out into the sunshine, colours reflected from the stained-glass windows onto his bald head. The man looked a similar age to the lady. He shook the vicar's hand vigorously and helped the lady along the path toward where Ian was sitting.

Ian tried to recall where he knew them from. They weren't from the village, he was sure of that, but he had definitely seen them somewhere before. He remembered her eyes. Kind. Forgiving. As they shuffled toward him, Ian noticed that the man was wearing a purple waistcoat. Ian looked away. Instead, he turned his attention to pulling at the grass from the ground beneath him.

"Hello, Ian," said the lady from a few feet away. Ian looked up. The man in the purple waistcoat had his arm around the her. It suddenly felt disrespectful to continue the conversation from the grass, so Ian quickly got to his feet, brushing the loose pieces of grass from the back of his trousers.

"Er, hello?" Ian smiled.

"It's been a long time," said the old lady. Her voice was gentle, almost sweet. She took Ian's hand in hers. It was cold. The man in the purple waistcoat placed his hand lightly on Ian's shoulder. He smiled. There was a sadness in his eyes.

"It has," said Ian. He hoped that his tone might compel the lady to introduce herself and save him the embarrassment of having to admit that he didn't exactly know who she was.

"You're not entirely sure who I am, are you?" she said. Ian noticed her eyes again, a spectrum of a million blues combining to make one deep blue that he had never seen before. They were perfect, like glass, and they seemed to be following every contour of his face.

"No," Ian admitted. "I'm sure we've met before. But I –"

"I'll save you the time, dear," said the lady. "I'm your grandmother."

"Okay," said Ian, in a tone that suggested 'Go on...' or 'Please continue'. He was embarrassed that was the best he could manage.

"Your father's mother," she said, and turned to the man in the purple waistcoat. "And this is Alan."

Ian stared out of the window.

The train was picking up speed and the fields that his family owned were quickly becoming a blur. He was now regretting buying a return ticket so early in the afternoon. He had enjoyed the conversation with his grandmother and wished that they'd had longer than the brief fifteen minutes to which the train had limited him. He wondered whether he had come across as rude by leaving so quickly. It had been kind of Alan to offer to drive him back to his university town. Alan had repeatedly said that it was on their way home, but Ian wasn't so sure. It seemed a little too convenient. Yes, it would have been nice to talk for a little longer with them, but two hours trapped in a car – especially on a hot day like today – may have been too much.

The brief encounter with his grandmother – or Louisa, as she had insisted he call her – had created something of a conundrum. Especially as he had already made the decision that he was going to have nothing further to do with the family. Louisa appeared very nice, very polite, very together. Very un-Perkins. She seemed genuinely interested in what Ian was doing and said that she had missed him at least three times in their short conversation. He suspected she was in her eighties, perhaps nineties; he wasn't good with ages. She had told him that she had known from the start that he wouldn't turn out like the "typical Perkins men". He had an idea but wasn't entirely sure what this meant, and it didn't seem like the time to interrogate her. The problem was that her short and somewhat vague statements opened up numerous possibilities within Ian's mind.

The loud horn of the train sounded and shattered Ian's thoughts. As the train rattled through a tunnel, Ian questioned whether he should even spend any more time thinking about Louisa's words. On the one hand, he was sufficiently intrigued in what she had to say. And she was family, after all. On the other hand, she had paid him no attention for his entire life. She had never sent a birthday card or telephoned at Christmas. In fact, he had only seen her once before, as she had reminded him: the day of Uncle Stephen's funeral.

He was also reminded about the information his father had given him. Louisa and Alan weren't nice people. They had attacked Dad, beaten him and left him alone in the farm. Louisa may have appeared to be a concerned, gentle old lady, but Ian was not stupid. He knew, especially from his family, that first impressions could be deceptive, that most people wear a mask and at some time it slips.

But a single comment that Alan had made just before they left nagged at Ian. It was almost a throwaway comment, said in a matter-of-fact way, with no bitterness or malice – just a simple statement that as far as he knew, the curse had now taken its youngest victim. Louisa had then leaned in and kissed Ian, her hair feeling like cardboard against his face. She had looked deep into his eyes and made him promise to come and see her. Ian had made the promise and taken the hand that Alan offered, shaking it firmly. He had then left them there, walked down the steps and out of the graveyard.

He was already deliberating whether he would keep the promise. He would discuss it with Rachel when he arrived back home. He was sure that she would have some helpful advice to offer. He reached into his bag and pulled out his CD player and put his headphones on.

He didn't know at that moment that he would keep his promise.

But not for many, many years.

TWENTY-EIGHT

"Hello," Ian whispered back.

The boy grinned. For a moment, they stared at one another. The boy looked like he was waiting for some instruction from Ian. For Ian to say something else.

Ian lay for a moment, looking down the length of his body, between his feet, to where the shape of the boy was. It was too dark to make out any of the boy's features in detail. His head throbbed. He clawed the duvet away from his face and rolled over and switched on the bedside lamp. It cast a dim light over one half of the room. The other half drowned in a treacle-like blackness. He rubbed his eyes, sat up and stared down the bed. The boy was gone.

Although the temperature in the room was normal, Ian felt cold. He got up and went to the drawers at the end of the bed where he rummaged around in the darkness. After a few moments, he retrieved his pyjama bottoms and a T-shirt and pulled them on.

"Hello," said the boy.

He giggled.

Ian turned quickly. The boy was sitting on the duvet opposite to where Ian had been lying. Rachel's side. The light didn't fully reach him and he sat in semi-darkness. Ian could see the boy's legs were crossed and he had one finger over his mouth, showing that he wanted Ian to be quiet. Without taking his eyes off the boy, Ian moved a few feet and reached across to the wall near the door. If this was real, he wanted to see it all. He pushed the switch and the ceiling light came on. Five bulbs. Three out. The darkness disappeared.

The boy remained. He pulled his finger away from his mouth.

"Hello," he said again. Then he laughed, and replaced his finger. He continued to grin.

Ian just stared.

He estimated the boy was no more than five years old. He was wearing a faded pyjama top, red and blue horizontal stripes with red arms. His pyjama bottoms were plain, navy-blue. On his feet were dark-blue slippers. A plastic emblem of Spiderman was stitched on the front of each. He had blond hair cut in a straightforward bowl haircut. Ian was drawn to the little boy's cheeks, which reminded him of two rosy-red apples. Such were their size that when the little boy smiled, they seemed to close his eyes, giving him an angelic, almost blissful appearance. And the boy hadn't stopped smiling once.

"Hello," he said between removing and replacing his finger. He giggled again. Ian smiled.

"Do you want me to be quiet?" Ian said quietly.

The boy shook his head and his hair danced like horses on a fairground ride.

"What do you want me to do?" Ian said, taking a step closer.

The boy's eyes opened wide and he pulled his shoulders up

209

alongside his cheeks. A shrug of sorts.

"Do you want to play?" asked Ian.

The boy shook his head and frowned slightly. He took his finger away from his mouth.

"Can I sit with you?" Ian said, taking another step. He was at the foot of the bed.

The boy solemnly shook his head again. And then his face brightened, and he slid down from the side of the bed. He pushed his thumb into his mouth and walked the few steps to Ian. He slipped his tiny hand inside Ian's and begin to lead him towards the door. Ian walked with him. The little boy removed his thumb and pulled the bedroom door open. Ian heard the clack-clack sound of the little boy sucking his thumb again as he led him across the landing.

The boy stopped outside the door of the bedroom that looked directly over the front garden of the house. Ian's childhood bedroom. He extracted his hand from Ian's and pointed at the door handle. This one was too high for him to reach. Ian opened the door and switched on the light. He hadn't been in this room for many months. His bed still remained, albeit now standing on its end against the wall. Everything else was, in his opinion at least, pretty much junk. There were storage boxes packaged up and sealed with parcel tape stacked on top of one another. Five or six black sacks, filled with clothes that used to fit either Rachel or Harry, were scattered randomly around the room. Months before, Rachel had assured Ian that she would sell them online. Now it seemed far more likely they would be given away to charity. Ian's old guitars and a few of Harry's toys rested against the wall behind the door.

The boy gripped Ian's little finger and led him on a path across the room through the black bags. Toward where the window hid behind the curtains. He began to suck his thumb with more intensity. And then, a few feet away from the window, he stopped, refusing to move forward any further. Ian looked down at the boy. He was staring directly forwards, through the curtains and the window into the garden.

"Do you want to look outside?" Ian asked.

Ian felt the boy grip his finger more tightly. The boy continued to stare, slowly nodding his head. It was slightly unnerving.

"Okay," said Ian, trying to sound playful, "let's have a look, shall we?"

He took a step forwards. Ian could feel the little boy shaking. He paused, and then pulled across the curtain quickly. Reflected in the window, he could see himself and the boy. The boy was crying. Giant tears rose over the crest of his cheeks and then dropped heavily to the floor. Ian crouched down and pulled the boy to him.

"It's okay," he said, stroking the boy's hair. "Don't cry."

The sobs became louder and Ian could feel the little boy shuddering as he pulled large gasps of air into his lungs. Ian suddenly felt very cold.

"What is it?" asked Ian. "What's the matter?"

The boy continued to cry. His intake of air was so deep that

Ian thought the skin in his throat may tear. The boy didn't speak.

"It's okay. It's okay," Ian whispered. "You're safe here."

Ian continued to stroke the boy's hair.

Soothing him with words of comfort.

Barely audible through the tears. Through the screams.

The boy broke free and pointed to the light. Ian went over and switched it off. The boy was sobbing heavily now. Although no sound left his mouth, Ian could hear his screams. The same screams he had dreamt about.

The little boy raised his finger and pointed to the garden.

"What's the matter?" said Ian as he walked over. "What is it?"

He reached the window and looked outside. The moon lit the horrific sight in the garden spectacularly. Beneath the foot of the tree, facing the house, were six open coffins. They had been perfectly arranged, equidistant from one another, like the markers on a clock – from three to nine.

Ian lost his balance for a moment. He was breathing heavily now. He closed his eyes and opened them again. Then he moved right up to the glass and looked more closely.

Three of the coffins were smaller than the others. Within each was a child. They could have been sleeping. Peaceful and still. Except one. It was a little boy. His eyes were wide open, alert like an animal the second before it is hit by a car. Startled. Fearful. His body was twisted awkwardly, the bones in his arms certainly broken. His tiny leg was bent backwards against his knee, his foot pointing to his face. And his face was enlarged, making it look abnormally big against the white satin of the coffin. Swollen and bruised.

The other three coffins were larger. In them lay adults, each with their eyes closed, their arms across their bodies, hands on opposite shoulders, their skin grey. At varying intervals, the shadows from the tree's branches crossed the coffins like bony fingers stroking the dead as they lay in the night air.

Ian cupped his hands to the window, trying to make out the faces of the dead. His nose pushed into the glass, but he couldn't see. They were too far away. Then he heard the scream. A long, high-pitched scream. He thought it had come from behind him. He spun to face the boy. But he was gone.

He heard it again, this time from outside.

Frantically, he turned back to the window.

The tree stood alone in front of him.

The coffins were gone.

TWENTY-NINE

Ian looked in the mirror. He knew before he even looked what to expect. And it was exactly that.

"Fuck," he said.

He looked terrible. Blackened skin entirely circled each sunken eye. Dark, heavy bags hung beneath them each eye. They reminded him of candle wax gathered over time around the sides of a bottle of wine. Ready to burst at any time. Ready to flood its dark contents down his cheeks. He pulled down his lower eyelashes to see his eyeballs clearly. The whites were instead a deep-pink. Red blood vessels zigzagged across like a lightning storm. He carefully peeled the plaster from his forehead and removed the toilet roll, which caused the wound to bleed. Using a flannel, he dabbed cold water on the wound to clean it. The cut was superficial, a bit deeper than a scratch. He dried it off and applied a further piece of tissue paper to stem the flow of blood. He raised and lowered his eyebrows, noticing the deep tracks across his forehead. For the first time he reminded himself of his father.

He wondered how long he had looked like this. Surely this couldn't have been a result of the previous night alone. Perhaps he had looked like this for some time; he couldn't remember the last time he had looked. Not properly. Come to think of it, he couldn't remember the last time he had even left the house. *It must be months*, he thought. *Months.*

His beard was now thick and unkempt. It was scattered with patches of brown hair, still clinging on to their colour, fighting the light grey and white hairs that had almost annexed his face. In all directions, numerous hairs tried to escape, breaking free from the mass and sticking out awkwardly. He ran his fingers through it, contemplating whether to just hack the whole thing off at that very moment. A new start. A new beginning. He reached down into the cupboard under the sink to retrieve his shaver. But when he returned to the mirror a moment later, he simply hadn't the energy. It would have to wait. There were more important things to do.

He turned on the tap and waited for the water to run cold. He took a large drink, gulping as the water splashed down into the sink. Then he cupped his hands and collected small pools, which he threw into his face repeatedly.

He went into the bedroom and checked his watch. It was still early, much too early to make the call. His eyes closed involuntarily. He fought to keep them open. He had so much to do, but he couldn't contemplate starting yet. He was just too tired; the weight of the previous night was sapping his energy. He decided to have a bath. That would waste some time.

For what seemed like the hundredth time that morning, Ian picked up his phone and checked the time. She must be awake by now. The bath had been totally unsuccessful; it had only made him feel more drained. In the end, after less than five minutes, he had got out, got dressed and come downstairs. He had spent the last two hours sitting in his usual seat at the kitchen table and staring down the length of the garden. Every few minutes, his head would nod toward the table and his eyes would close. Then he'd wake himself with an uncomfortable jolt, and it would take a second or two to remember who and where he was. He would check the time, stare outside and the situation would repeat.

He had consumed two cafetières of coffee in an attempt to keep himself awake. It wasn't working. He realised that sleep would be the best thing for him, but he simply didn't have time. He was getting so close now.

And getting to the truth would change everything.

The giant metal cogs would begin turning, tiny little movements at first, and the machine would awaken. And then, as steam passed through, each part would slowly come to life. The machine would finally chug back into motion, belying the fact that it had lain unused for so many months. Within minutes each part would be working in total synchronicity. Everything would return to how it had been, and at last his life could start again. Ian and Rachel could finally move on together, the synchronised machine they always were. Even though tiredness crippled his entire body, little spikes of adrenalin kept Ian going, reminding him he was near the finish line. He felt like he was close to finding some magic key that he could post into the lock and turn, and their life would be back.

He flipped over the phone again. It was near eight. He could wake her now. He had to tell her what had happened. Tell her just how close he was.

Rachel answered the phone before Ian had even heard it ring. It sounded like she was travelling. He asked if she was okay to speak. She was.

"Listen, I know you said not to ring, but I need you to come back. There's some really weird stuff, like *really* weird, that's been going on here." The words rattled like gunfire, falling into one another; there was no time for spaces in between. It may have been the caffeine.

"Ian, slow down," Rachel said.

"Okay, sorry," he said, "sorry, sorry, sorry."

"I'm already on my way back."

"Oh, okay." He was out of breath. "That's good. That's good. What time, er, when?"

"I'll be a few hours, okay?"

"Okay."

"You'll be okay till then?"

"Er, yeah, sure," Ian said, his voice accelerating again. "It's just that I need to tell you about –"

"Tell me when I get back, okay?"

"Yeah, sure. Yeah. Yeah, that's no problem. Er –"

"See you then, okay?"

And she was gone.

There was so much to do now. They'd be home soon.

Ian went upstairs to the bedroom and straightened the

duvet, plumped the pillows. He wasn't sure why. Inside the bedside drawer he was relieved to see the folded piece of paper he had put there the previous night. He pushed it into his jeans pocket and pulled out the study key.

He bounded downstairs and unlocked the study door. There were only a few hours before Rachel would be back. He knew that he wouldn't have time to finalise his research, but he could get that little bit closer. And that would mean that he would be closer to pulling the lever on the side of the machine and resuming his life. He decided that he wouldn't show Rachel the result of his work until he could prove beyond doubt that the curse did exist. There was no point in showing her what he had done so far; she wouldn't be interested. Just like she hadn't been interested when he had initially told her what he intended to do.

He remembered the day vividly. He had seen her from the lounge window sitting next to a watering can underneath the sycamore tree. She was sobbing, her gardening gloves partly covering her face. It was clear when he approached her that she didn't want to talk. She held up one of her gloved hands to stop him getting any closer. He noticed that she had trails of dirt on her cheeks.

"I saw you from the lounge," he said.

She didn't even look at him.

"I came to see if you were okay?"

She looked at him, her expression the epitome of disgust. "Yeah, Ian. I'm fine," she spat.

218

He paused for a moment and then went to take a step forward.

"Don't!" she screamed. "Don't even move."

He stopped.

"I used to love it here," she said quietly, "and now it's all ruined. You ruined it."

"I know," he said.

"Oh, you do? That's good. Because until now it's been some fucking curse."

"There is a curse."

"Jesus, Ian."

"I'll prove it."

"Just leave me alone, okay?"

"I will prove it to you, Rachel," he said resolutely.

The watering can skittled across the lawn, coming to a stop a few inches from where Ian was standing.

"Just go." She began crying. "Please."

Ian lifted the needle and dropped it onto the black record spinning below. There was a brief crackle and then guitars. The music would serve two purposes: increase his productivity, and increase his chance of staying awake. The unmistakable voice of Julian Casablancas began, and so did Ian. He took a slurp from his coffee and pulled the piece of paper from his pocket.

He unfolded it and laid it on the desk, flattening it with his hands. Immediately, he saw that it was different from the night before. Thick red crayon crosses had been added alongside some of the names. He couldn't recall doing that. In fact, he knew he hadn't done that. He scanned the names: his brother, his niece. A red cross had also been placed next to Uncle Stephen. This made sense, yet at the same time made no sense. Yes, he would expect the crosses alongside those names; they were all dead, after all. What made no sense was how the crosses had got there in the first place.

Even more confusing was the fact that there was no cross against his father's name. Dad had died more than a decade before. Ian had heard that the diagnosis had only been made right at the very end. The cancer had eaten away at him hungrily and finally disposed of him a few weeks later. That was all Ian knew. He hadn't attended the funeral. He had kept his promise, his commitment to leave the family behind. As for his mother, as far as he knew she was still in the nursing home they'd put her in when she couldn't remember her own name.

He stared at the other names with crosses on the paper. It was helpful that he could focus his work on those individuals first.

Though he

      could

        barely

          keep

            his

          eyes

        open.

He

had

to

press

on.

Get to the end.

The answer.

Perhaps it *was* him who had added the crosses. He really wasn't sure. Memories of the night before were already becoming muddled. He was wasting time. There wasn't time to think about this now. He had to get on.

Ian scanned the room and found the pile for his brother. He would start the next phase of his research here. It was vital that he found out when each of his family members had died and, perhaps more importantly, exactly how. Ian had not spoken to Stuart after his marriage. Of course, he had seen him at his niece's funeral, but they hadn't spoken. That was the last time he had seen Stuart. And now it was too late.

Ian felt slightly guilty that he didn't know more about his brother's death. After all, it had only been a few years earlier. He hadn't taken the time to find out any more than what he could read in the newspapers. Just as with Dad, Ian had kept his commitment to stay away from Stuart. At the time of his death they hadn't spoken for more than fifteen years. His single conversation with Gillian, if you could even call it that, was limited to the night of her marriage to Stuart. After Stuart's death, Ian's solicitor dealt with getting her out of the cottage

221

and removing all her possessions. End of story.

Ian sat down on the floor next to the small pile of papers and cuttings he had collected. He began to read.

It was difficult to focus.

His eyes closed.

He snapped them open.

He needed to read this.

The words moved around the page as his vision moved in and out of focus.

It was so hard to concentrate. At the end of a line his eyes would fail to move down to the next line and he would find himself rereading the same words again and again. The same two sentences, over and over.

Perkins, age 40, was found dead at his home yesterday. It appears he died from a single gunshot wound...Perkins, age 40, was found dead at his home yesterday. It appears he died from a single gunshot wound...Perkins, age 40, was found dead at his home yesterday. It appears he died from a single gunshot wound...Perkins, age 40, was found dead at his home yesterday. It appears he died from a single gunshot wound...Perkins, age 40, was found dead at his home yesterday. It appears he died from a single gunshot wound...Perkins, age 40, was found dead at his home yesterday. It appears he died from a single gunshot wound...Perkins, age 40, was found dead at his home yesterday. It appears he died from a single gunshot wound...Perkins, age 40, was found dead at his home yesterday. It appears he died from a single gunshot wound...Perkins, age 40, was found dead at his home yesterday. It appears he died from a single gunshot wound...

And over.

And over again.

He forced his eyes to open, but it was no good.

He was too tired.

There was a brief crackle and the needle lifted from the record. It clicked back into its resting place and the record gradually slowed down until it stopped.

Ian was already asleep.

THIRTY

"So that's it?" said Stuart.

He was sitting at the range table, staring down the garden.

"After all this?" He held his upturned hands in front of him, like he was holding an invisible beach ball.

"I've already told you, Stuart," said Gillian. She stood against the work surface. A safe distance away.

He slammed his fist down on the table. The salt and pepper jumped. "So you let me spend twenty grand on the kitchen, then you leave me?"

"Stuart," she said, "you know as well as I do, it's not about a bloody kitchen."

He turned to face her. "Well, what is it about then?"

"I've already told you. I'm not going through it again."

"So that's it? You leave me for him. End of?"

"Yes. That's it."

"Right," he said, struggling to sound firm. "You'd better go then."

"I'll be back after lunch tomorrow, to collect some of my things. It'd probably be better for us both if you weren't here."

She picked up her car keys from the work surface and walked out into the hall. Stuart heard the front door gently close behind her. His life had just left the house.

He stood and walked across the kitchen to the cupboard

in the corner just to the left of the sink. Like every night, he pulled open the door and collected a bottle of bourbon from the top shelf. Then he took a small whisky glass and returned to his position at the range table. He unscrewed the top and poured the golden liquid, half-filling the glass. To save time, he swigged a mouthful straight from the bottle. Then he swallowed and opened his mouth wide, sucking in cool air to alleviate the burning sensation in his throat. He wiped his mouth on his checked shirt sleeve.

And then he reached for the glass and threw back the whisky. He poured another, drank it down and poured another. His mind turned to the last three hours of conversation with Gillian. She had used the same words, dressed them up and then repeated them each time in a different way. The outcome was very simple: firstly, she no longer wanted to be with him, and secondly, she had found somebody else. It seemed to Stuart that the first revelation had been thrown in to soften the blow of the second. She had found the new man at the library where she volunteered on Wednesdays and Fridays. It had been going on for some time. She hadn't meant for it to happen, but it had. She had been very firm and matter of fact about it. Her speech seemed very polished, like she had practised in the mirror, in the car, whenever he hadn't been around.

It was completely unexpected. They had been married for more than twenty years, and as far as Stuart could see, nothing had changed. They spent most Friday and Saturday evenings in the village, drinking in the two local pubs – seven until nine thirty in the Ploughman, then next door to the Star and Rose from nine thirty until...well, it could be gone midnight, sometimes later. They holidayed twice a year, on the Greek island that they both liked. Where they knew the bar staff and the waiters. Where they liked the food. Where they were always greeted with open arms every other night at the Red Lion's quiz night. They holidayed at the same time each year – just before the harvest season and then immediately after.

Stuart had, of course, tried to question Gillian, tried to persuade her that she was making a mistake. But she had an answer for everything. Didn't he understand what she was saying? She was unhappy. She had met someone new. It was time to move on. Simple as that. She wanted half of everything. That was fair, she said. The conversation had continued like a ceiling fan, rotating back to the same point over and over again. He had to face it. It was over. She was going. Going. Gone.

Stuart took another drink and ran his fingers through his knotted hair. She wanted half? Half of what? Without her, there was nothing anyway. He pulled his phone from his pocket and called her. The line rang once and then stopped. He tried again: the same. And again. She was rejecting his calls. He needed to talk to her. There must be some resolution to this, something he could do. He poured another drink.

What was it she had said about his drinking? It was out of control. Was that what she'd said? Sure, he liked a whisky or two when he got in each night, but he deserved it. He was up at six every morning, in at seven. Why wouldn't he relax with a drink or two? They had no children, no responsibilities aside from the farm, and once work was over for the day, a drink was his reward. That was hardly out of control, was it? Jesus, she liked a drink as well. Well, he'd show her, he thought. *Out of control? We'll see.* He drank down the remainder of his glass and unscrewed the lid of the bottle again. As he drew it to his mouth, his phone vibrated on the table. It was her. He put the bottle down and lifted the phone.

"Hello?" he said.

"Why are you ringing? I told you not to call."

"Well, I was just thinking that, er, maybe I wanted to talk about us."

"Have you been drinking?"

The question caught Stuart off-guard. His brain wasn't quick enough to form a response.

"You have, haven't you? I can tell from your voice, Stuart. Jesus."

"I had a couple."

"It's always a couple, isn't it? Don't you listen to anything I say to you? For Christ's sake, Stuart, you need help. Seriously."

He had heard that line so many times before.

"Listen, I told you. Don't call me. I'll be back tomorrow afternoon for my things. Do *not* be there."

She was gone.

Stuart threw the phone down onto the table. He picked up the bottle and drank it back, mouthful by mouthful. Liquid escaped around the edges of his mouth, running down his cheeks and onto his neck. He slammed the bottle back onto the table, denting the surface. He grabbed his phone and pressed her name again. Her phone was switched off. That really was it. There was nothing more he could do. She had taken his life. He stood and immediately steadied himself against the wall.

The room was moving slightly, and as he stumbled toward the French windows, he swept a couple of pictures from the wall with his shoulder. He made it to the doors and pushed them open. It was warm outside, and he squinted in the sun as he made his way unsteadily past the kitchen window toward the barn. He staggered along the small stone path, unintentionally trampling the flowerbeds on either side, crushing the small flowers beneath his work boots. He made it to the door of the barn, which was already open. Sunlight beamed through two holes in the roof. Replacement slates were on his list. His never-ending list of things to do.

He edged his way inside, using the wall of the barn to keep himself upright. The barn was almost full, stacked high with straw wrapped in cream plastic. He left the relative safety of the barn wall and ventured to the small table a few metres away. He nearly fell, but caught himself just in time, grabbing hold of the back of the chair. He was out of breath. He slumped down onto the seat, facing the door.

From the table, he collected the shotgun he had been using earlier that morning. Wild rabbits had been on the receiving end. He pulled the latch, opening the barrel. It was empty. He pushed his hand deep in his jacket pocket, looking for a cartridge. He always kept one or two on him. His pockets were full of receipts, other bits of paper, screws, nails, tree ties. His fingers felt and discarded each item. And there it was, the smooth cylinder. Just the one. He pulled it from his jacket and tried to post it into the barrel, which moved and blurred in front of his eyes. The alcohol was making it hard for his hands to do what his brain was telling them. He tried again and again, the cartridge catching on the breech or missing it entirely, and then finally it was in. He clicked the break-action shut and lowered the gun to the floor.

He leaned forwards and fed the barrel into his mouth, keeping his thumb on the trigger. The metal dug into the roof of his mouth, right at the back. He pulled the trigger. Just a click. A tiny click. He looked down, momentarily confused. Then he removed the gun from his mouth and through narrowed eyes located the safety catch and clicked it off. The last sound he would hear. He pushed the barrel firmly under his chin and squeezed the trigger.

It wasn't until around lunchtime the next day that Stuart Perkins was found. Gillian arrived exactly on time to collect her belongings. She found the house unlocked, and when she walked through into the kitchen the French windows were gently swinging in the breeze. She followed the path to the doorway of the barn, past the trampled flowerbeds. As she reached the barn door, she saw her husband's lifeless body on the floor. From where she was standing, it took her a moment to realise that the pool of sticky-looking liquid on the floor surrounded the space where his head used to be. Behind him, the large wall of cream plastic was decorated with an artistic fountain of maroon blood and pieces of greyish brain matter.

Alongside him lay his gun.

And his faithful dog.

Solemnly staring at her.

His teeth, and the fur around his mouth, also covered in maroon.

THIRTY-ONE

"Daddy!"

Ian opened his eyes. Harry was already on top of him. His arms were wrapped around his neck, his temple pushed firmly against Ian's. His breath smelled of sweets. Ian pulled himself up from the floor into a sitting position, Harry still attached. He strategically moved Harry's brown boot from his groin. That felt better. He squeezed him. It had felt like forever since he had seen him.

"Hello, son," Ian whispered repeatedly into his ear. It was good to hold him. Good to smell him.

Eventually, he uncoupled Harry's arms and stood him on the floor in front of him. He scanned him, looking at each feature, each hair on his head, checking to see whether he had changed in the last few days. Harry's little face beamed, a secret smile. The sun seemed to shine from behind his eyes. Ian rubbed the sleep from his own eyes and silently yawned. God, it was good to see Harry. He hadn't realised just how much he had missed him. He made everything worthwhile.

Harry's face suddenly dropped. "Oh dear, Daddy."

"What's the matter?" Ian said.

"Is Daddy hurt?"

"No," Ian said, "I've just been sleeping. Daddy's just tired."

"No," Harry insisted, pointing with his finger, "Daddy hurt."

Ian must have looked confused, because Harry leaned forward and pushed firmly into the cut on Ian's forehead. It stung.

"Oh, that," Ian said. "No, it's okay. Don't worry. It's nothing."

"Ooouch," said Harry, pointing again.

A spot of blood dripped onto the papers next to Ian. He wiped his forehead with the back of his hand. The red streak seemed to concern Harry more. He looked like he may cry.

"It's okay, Harry."

His lip quivered.

"I just need to get some toilet roll," said Ian, getting to his feet.

"I'll get toilet roll," said Harry, suddenly pleased he could help. He turned and tottered to the door.

"That's very kind of you, Harry," Ian called after him.

A few moments later, Harry was pushing toilet roll into Ian's hand. Ian could see the trail going out of the door behind Harry to where the rest of the roll no doubt remained, attached to the wall. He smiled.

"Thanks, Harry," he said, wiping the wound.

"I *can* do it myself, you know, Daddy," said Harry, standing with his hands on his hips. He looked just like his mother.

"I'm sure you can."

Harry looked around the room and noticed for the first time the toilet roll that had followed him in. "Oh no," he sighed, shaking his head, "more paper."

They spent the next ten minutes talking about what Harry

had been doing with Mummy all week. Harry informed Ian that they had been to the park and to the zoo and even to McDonald's. Grandma had come too. Then, abruptly, Harry decided that they had talked enough. He was going to find his toys. He turned as he reached the study door.

"Will Daddy play with me later on?" he asked.

"Of course," Ian said, "when I've spoken to Mummy."

"Okay, Daddy. I love you."

"I love you too, son. More than anything."

"Even all this paper?" Harry giggled.

Ian laughed. "Much more than this paper."

Rachel had just left the bathroom when Ian reached the bottom of the stairs. He caught a glimpse of her, just a passing moment, as she moved across the landing, her body covered by a large white towel. As he made it to the top, her bedroom door was just closing. It clicked behind her. Ian noticed the lock and key leaning against the skirting board just outside the door. Time had overtaken him, and he was annoyed that he had completely forgotten to repair it while she was away. He hoped that she wouldn't be angry. Something inside told him his hope was misguided.

Although he hadn't had a chance to speak to Rachel since she returned, it somehow didn't feel appropriate to hang around outside her bedroom door while she was getting ready. Hovering around her, chivvying her along, was always a sure-fire way to start an argument. He'd learned the hard way that when she was getting ready for a night out, staying downstairs was his best option. Well out of the way.

Actually, it was a long time since they'd had a night out anywhere.

He resisted knocking on her door. He would present his research to her over a meal, when he had her full attention. That was a good idea. Some posh restaurant somewhere, maybe near her mother's. That way they'd have a babysitter. A nice meal and a bottle of wine, and he could tell her the exact reason he'd been in the study all that time. When he finished, she would realise that none of this was his fault. He would be exonerated and they'd leave the restaurant arm in arm, in love again. How they were before.

And he'd be willing to forgive too. He was sure that he'd be able to overcome the anger and bitterness that she had unfairly directed towards him. He could remember the way she was before, the woman he married. He would allow her mistake to pass. He'd happily wipe the slate clean.

He turned to go back downstairs. He'd mention the meal to Rachel when she was dressed. As he reached the top of the stairs, he stopped at Harry's bedroom door. Making sure that he couldn't be seen, he peered through the crack of the door. Harry was lying on his tummy on the floor. His legs were bent at the knees and he was kicking his feet absentmindedly. Ian couldn't see exactly what he was doing, so he pushed the door open a little further. He could now see the back of Harry's head. On the rug in front of him was an open colouring book. In his right hand he was holding a crayon and carefully colouring in the picture. He suddenly turned.

"Are you watching, Daddy?" He smiled.

"Yes, sorry."

Harry raised his eyebrows.

"I just wanted to know whether you wanted to play now," Ian lied.

"No, thank you very much indeed," Harry said. "I'm colouring in."

He held up the picture, a bright-red fire engine with an uncoloured ladder on the top. "Do you like it?" he said.

"Yes," said Ian, impressed that Harry hadn't coloured outside the lines. "I do."

"Thanks, Daddy. You can leave me in lots of peace now."

Ian smiled.

"Okay. See you later."

Ian pulled the door, leaving a slight gap. He watched for a moment longer. It was good to have Harry back.

THIRTY-TWO

As it happened, Rachel never did leave her room that night. Ian waited for more than an hour in the lounge, absentmindedly flicking through the TV channels, anticipating the sound of her feet coming down the stairs. Frustrated that he was wasting time, he decided to continue his work in the study. He was close now. So close.

Soon he was surrounded by paperwork. Making notes. Scribbling down family connections. Dates. Times. Circumstances. He had to be prepared. Tomorrow was a big day. He expected that at some time during the evening, once she was ready, he would turn and see her standing in the doorway. But that time never came, and it wasn't until the next morning that he got the opportunity to speak to her.

A new day, and he felt good. For the first time that week he had managed a full night's sleep: no nightmares, no screams, no interruptions. He was thankful for that. He woke feeling refreshed, ready for what he had to do. Today he would insert the final piece in the jigsaw. And once it was in, at long last Rachel would be able to see the whole picture.

He showered and dressed, excitedly buttoning up his shirt. He wanted to look like he had made an effort. He decided that he wouldn't tell Rachel where he was going; at this stage she didn't need to know. He would tell her once he was sure that he had all the answers. When they were sitting opposite one another sipping expensive wine, their faces lit only by candlelight. Just the two of them. When he could feel the love growing between them as he told her his story, from the beginning. All about his research and his journey. And of course, the truth that he had discovered. His heart sank. His job. Hmm. He wasn't looking forward to telling her about that at all. He put it to the back of his mind. Today was much more important. Perhaps he'd leave telling her about the job for another day.

When he entered the lounge, Rachel was lying on the sofa, staring at the ceiling. There was an open book resting across her chest. He sat on the arm of the chair opposite her.

"Hey," he said.

"Hey."

"What're you up to?"

"Dunno," she said. "Just reading, I suppose."

"Surprised you can see the words," he joked, nodding towards the position of the book.

She smiled a weak, sarcastic smile.

"So, how was it at your mum's?"

"It was okay, thanks. We did lots. Got lots of sleep as well."

"Good."

"Is she okay?"

"Who?"

"Your mum."

"Yeah, she's fine, thanks."

"Good."

Rachel took the book from her chest and placed it on the floor. She sat up at the end of the sofa. "Listen, Ian. We need to talk."

"Right," he said.

"No, I mean properly. Come and sit down."

"Can this wait?"

"Why?"

"It's just" – he nodded toward the window – "there's something I need to do."

"What?"

"I need to nip out. In the car."

"Well, this is important."

"Is it about us?"

"Yes."

"If it's okay, can we talk later? We've got all day. I won't be long."

Rachel sighed.

"Well, where are you going?"

"I just need to use the car."

"What for?"

"I just need to go out for a bit, okay?"

"Okay, I suppose."

"Thanks. We'll talk later, yeah?"

Rachel picked up her book. She opened it and began to read. Ian took it as his signal to leave. He walked toward the door.

"Why are you dressed like that?" she said without looking

up.

Ian stopped. "Like what?"

"Smart."

"Just thought I'd wear a shirt for a change." It didn't sound convincing.

Rachel screwed her face up.

Ian waited for her to speak again. When she didn't, he left. As he reached the car he heard the faint sound of the phone ringing inside the house. He'd leave it for Rachel to deal with. He had far too much to do.

It truly was a perfect day. The sun shone brightly down on the car. The windscreen flickered bright then dull, as the car passed beneath the heavy overhang of trees that lined the roads. And then, when the flickering became almost too distracting and Ian feared that the car may leave the road, the countryside opened up and the warmth of the sun filled the car.

Ian lowered his window. He estimated that it would be about an hour's drive to the nursing home. It had taken several telephone calls over the previous week to ascertain whether Louisa was, in fact, still alive. The brown envelope containing the old photographs had been the key. Deep inside had been a small slip of paper. On the paper, in large light-green lettering, had been the words 'With Compliments'. And to the right had been the name and address of the nursing home: Tall Trees. The irony was not lost on Ian.

He had excitedly dialled the telephone number, only to find

that it no longer worked. The area codes had changed in the two decades since the paper had been printed. It had taken a few moments online to establish that the nursing home was still in existence, and he had tentatively telephoned to see whether his relation was still a resident, and indeed still alive. His initial difficulty was that he wasn't sure which relative he was calling about. The nursing home was not about to hand out details of all its residents. It had taken a few more hours of research and one or two less-than-honest phone calls to get the nursing home to admit that Louisa Perkins, his grandmother, was still there.

Exactly an hour later, the sat-nav announced that Ian had arrived. He slowed the car to a stop alongside a high stone wall which ran around the perimeter of his destination. From where he was, it was impossible to see any buildings on the other side. The walls were surrounded by nothing but open fields in all directions. In the distance, Ian could see one or two properties dotted about the landscape.

He edged the car along slowly until he came to the entrance of the nursing home. A narrow drive dissected the long stone wall, which curved inwards at either side of it. There was an old wooden sign attached to the wall, the green lettering peeling away from the cream background. It read simply, 'Tall Trees'. He took a deep breath. The gravel cracked under his tyres as he pulled the car into the drive.

The drive was flanked by small wooden posts, each attached to the next with a plastic white chain. The brightness of the day was immediately extinguished by huge trees and oversized

240

shrubs that threatened to swallow the car. Such was the darkness that the car activated its own lights. Ian pulled the button to close the car window. The drive twisted one way then the other, and Ian had to drive slowly to ensure that he didn't destroy the little wooden fence. Thick foliage stroked either side of the car, which reminded him of being in a car wash.

After half a mile of driving at less than walking pace, he came to a yellow-and-black-striped barrier. To his right was a small sentry box. The box was painted in the same cream as the sign at the front. It was in a similar state. The paint was blistered and peeling and covered with green moss along the sides that were facing him. The car lights illuminated the seat inside – rotted away, its once horizontal seat still joined in the middle but now forming a V shape. The box was empty.

It was dark inside the car, and Ian flicked on the light. He waited for a few moments for the barrier to open.

Nothing.

He looked around to see whether there was a button to push and microphone to speak into to alert the nursing home that he had arrived. There was nothing obvious, unless the trees and shrubs had swallowed it. Then, on the other side of the barrier diagonally opposite him, he spotted a small grey box. Perhaps that was it. That would make sense for those leaving but not those arriving. He pondered getting out of the car. Something about the trees surrounding him made him think twice. It was so dark, even with the lights on. He imagined that as soon as he left the car something bad would happen. Something

241

otherworldly.

The events at the cottage over the last few weeks had opened his mind to this kind of thing again. For many years he had managed to lock away the feelings from his childhood. But now, they were back. Disconcerting, almost sinister feelings. A feeling of being watched, his every move under somebody's microscope. When he was younger, he'd had that feeling often: invisible eyes following his walk across the landing or watching as he lay in bed. It had been easier to put these experiences down to childhood immaturity. But everything he had recently experienced felt real. Like somebody *was* watching. That it wasn't just the result of a fervent imagination hungry for answers.

He hooked his fingers around the handle to open the door. He told himself he was being ridiculous. The catch clicked, and he pushed the door open slightly with his forearm. Freezing air rushed into the car, biting his skin. And as it did, the barrier woke from its slumber and began to lift. Ian quickly pulled the door closed and pushed the lock. The barrier jerked slowly upwards, resting every few inches.

Ian watched until the barrier was high enough to clear the car. Then he put the car into first gear and continued his crawl along the lane. Within fifty feet, the trees finished and the little picket fence opened wide, sweeping around a large, almost empty car park. Ahead of him stood an enormous building, built from huge slabs of stone that had been blackened by the elements over the years and with huge sash windows lining the entire upper floor. It reminded him of the disused mental institution that characters are warned against visiting in the horror films he had watched. Between the sash windows on the ground floor, wide stone steps gradually narrowed on their climb toward the large red doorway that led into the home.

THIRTY-THREE

Rachel stood by the window, staring down the lawn toward the main road. No matter which direction she looked in, her eyes were always drawn back to the tree. It was impossible to escape. It stood over the house grimly, its giant branches stretching out almost as wide as the cottage itself. Open arms, like those of someone expectantly awaiting a lover on a station platform. But these arms were not welcoming; they were something altogether more sinister.

These were the open arms of ownership.

The arms of control.

Her eyes switched to the branch that pointed toward the house. Stripped of bark, it was a long finger beckoning her toward the tree, pulling her in. Ready to take another victim.

She sighed and turned away. She couldn't bear to look at it anymore. She felt like going outside and destroying it once and for all. Taking an axe and hacking into its thick trunk until it was no more. Obliterating it.

In fact, at the end of the previous summer she and Ian had made enquiries about having it removed. Nothing would have pleased them more than seeing the trunk sliced neatly into circular pieces and driven away from the cottage. But it wasn't possible. The tree was protected under some statute and there were severe penalties for removing it. Fines that would have bankrupted them. And anyway, nobody in the area would even take on the work; they would lose their livelihood.

Even if she and Ian had been allowed to take down the tree, Rachel expected that it would have resisted. She imagined that as they sawed angles of wood from the trunk, it would magically self-heal, the wood reappearing in front their eyes. The tree would stand firm, would not allow itself to be defeated. She imagined it shaking violently to ward off anyone who dared to challenge its omnipotence.

She sat down in her usual place in the kitchen and idly flicked through a magazine. Ian had been gone for well over two hours now and the waiting was killing her. She had built herself up for this conversation over the last few weeks and now, when she was finally ready to talk, to *properly talk*, he was gone.

The last week had really helped to organise her mind. Since the previous summer she had seriously questioned whether she was going mad. Coping with her own feelings was difficult enough, but the experience was made so much more difficult by the way Ian had been acting. At the turn of the year, a few weeks after the doctor finally prescribed her medication, she had felt that she was beginning to cope with everything a little better. They were tiny steps, but nevertheless they signified progress, a glimmer in the unending darkness. But at that time, Ian had begun to act more and more strangely. He didn't seem to be coping with their situation at all. It was almost as if he didn't accept that any of it was happening – living his life, denying the fact that their marriage was crumbling right in front of them. In the early days, she had tried to talk to him so many times, but there was simply no getting through. He avoided her.

Then the screams began. The first time it happened, her heart had beaten so fast that she honestly felt she was going to die, that her heart was going to explode.

They had both been asleep when she was woken by his whispering. She remained still, and watched him through one eye, the other deep into the pillow. He was propped up on one arm, and he seemed to be whispering to somebody at the end of their bed. She couldn't make out what he was saying, but it appeared he was having a conversation. He would whisper and then stop as if awaiting a response. A few moments later he would smile or nod his head eagerly, and then she'd see his mouth move again with hushed, indecipherable words. She watched for a while and then closed her eyes, assuming that he was simply talking in his sleep.

Then Ian gripped her shoulders and began frantically shaking her. Her eyes snapped open and he was there, his face inches from hers, screaming her name repeatedly. "Rachel, Rachel, Rachel!" At times the screams were so loud that his voice failed him and no words came out, or her name was broken partway through. He shook her hard, his grip too tight to wriggle free. He pulled her up toward him and then slammed her back into the bed. Then he pulled her up and did it again. Within moments, her strength was gone. Her body flopped in his hands and he smashed her into the bed again. Without the softness of the mattress beneath her, she would have been unconscious, if not dead, within three or four movements. The screaming continued, her name over and over. She became dizzy, disoriented as he slammed her down again. The skin on her upper arms reddened, sore from his grip.

And then she felt his grip relax and he stopped. She saw her opportunity and rolled over and landed heavily on the bedroom floor. Then, naked, she scrambled backwards along the floor until she was resting against the wall. Panting. Gasping for breath. That was when she felt sharp pains run through her chest and believed that at this moment her heart had given in.

A few feet away on the bed, Ian was asleep. Purring gently.

She had slept in the spare room that night. The next day Ian had no recollection and she believed him. He seemed genuinely perplexed by the story she told him.

A few nights later it happened again.

And then again.

And then the spare room – complete with lock – became her sanctuary.

Rachel pushed herself back from the kitchen table, stretching her arms out as far as they would reach. It was impossible to settle.

She checked the clock on the wall again.

The speech she had practised began to circle inside her head again. She needed to get it out. She didn't want their marriage to end. She had made her vows and committed to Ian, and she meant them. Over the last few months they had, of course, been stretched to snapping point, but she wasn't about to give up. Ian was a good man; her mother had reminded her of that. He just needed help. Whilst away from the cottage, she had spent hours taking seemingly endless walks. And she had slowly been able to pull the characteristics of Ian she loved back to the front of her mind. She wanted it to work, but she couldn't listen to any more of his delusions. His talk of visions. His conversations with invisible children. His endless research into his family history, in search of answers that weren't there.

And the imaginary curse.

No more. She had finished with humouring him months before. It was easier just not to speak, to ignore him and hope that over time he'd get through it. People always said that time made things easier: "Give it some time. He'll be alright in time." Not in this case. Ian had got worse and worse and worse. Too much time had passed, and time – the great healer – was threatening to destroy Rachel's husband. She needed to have this conversation with him.

Today. This minute. Now.

If she didn't, then she agreed with her mother's grim prophecy: that Rachel would go the same way that Ian had.

She needed him home right this second.

And he needed to accept help.

Urgently.

THIRTY-FOUR

Ian tried the large brass handle in the centre of the red door. He quickly realised that from this side it served no purpose, aside from a means to pull the door shut. Which was exactly how it was now. He noticed a small golden plaque engraved simply with the word 'Visitors' and a little arrow pointing to a doorbell. He pushed the doorbell and waited. A moment later he heard the noise of static, followed by a male voice. Deep and monotone.

"Yes?"

"Oh, hello. I've come to visit."

"Who?"

"My grandmother."

"Name, please?" The speaker sounded frustrated.

"Louisa Perkins."

"Your name?"

"It's Ian. Ian Perkins."

There was a slight hum and the door clicked open. Ian imagined a tall, bald, hunched man dressed as a butler on the other side, a vision from a 1930s' Dracula film. He was wrong. Inside, he was greeted by a grand entrance hall painted blandly in a clinical mint colour. The walls were bare, the original picture rail unused. There was a small coffee table surrounded on two sides by garish green sofas. In the corner was a reception desk. Behind it was a door.

Ian leaned on the reception desk and placed his plastic folder down. He was about to ring the small metal bell when the door opened. A young-looking girl wearing a uniform that matched the walls came through. She smiled.

"Mr Perkins?" she said.

Ian confirmed his name and the girl asked him for his identification. She was very apologetic and told him that this wasn't something they would ask for next time he visited. It was company policy, she said. She also told him that she couldn't remember the last time Mrs Perkins had been visited.

"Does she know I'm here?" Ian asked, putting his driving licence back into the folder.

"She does," the girl said. "She was very surprised."

"Did she remember me?"

"Oh, yes. Her face lit up."

Ian took a seat, as requested. It was unusually quiet. He leafed through a magazine. Moments later the door opened again and a man appeared. He announced, in a booming, deep voice, that he would take Ian upstairs.

They walked up the grand staircase together. Ian asked several questions about the age of the building, but the man didn't seem interested in engaging in conversation. Instead, an awkward silence hung in the air momentarily and then scurried quickly back down the stairs.

At the top of the stairs, they turned to the right and walked along the landing to the first door on the left. The man stopped so abruptly that Ian nearly banged into him. He turned and informed Ian that Mrs Perkins was their eldest resident and that she had been at Tall Trees longer than any other resident.

More than twenty years.

And in that time he couldn't remember her ever having a visitor.

The man knocked lightly on the door and pushed it open. His head disappeared and a moment later he informed Ian that he could go in. The man held the door open for Ian and then gently closed it behind him.

Ian looked around the room. It was enormous. The ceilings seemed to stretch upwards forever. The walls were decorated in a dark red – almost burgundy – wallpaper patterned with slightly lighter red leaves and branches. A large mahogany dining table with eight matching chairs stood near the door. Ian noticed that two places had been set, each complete with silver knives and forks and a blood-red napkin. The table was finished with a large silver candelabra with three red candles. He could see they had never been lit. At the end of the table was a door, slightly ajar. Through it, Ian could see a large bed, with a metal headboard. Vertical poles like prison bars guarding the pillows.

Ian walked around the table to the lounge area. Two large maroon sofas formed one half of a square facing an unlit open fire. A large painting hung above the fire, and to either side enormous windows overlooked the car park. To his left, in a high-backed chair, sat a woman. Ian smiled and nodded as he made his way around the back of a sofa. He stood awkwardly for a moment, and she signalled with her hand for him to be seated. He sat on the end of the sofa nearest to her and placed his folder next to him.

The woman was sitting upright, rigid, her thick legs planted firmly on the floor. Small, black, patent court shoes crumpled her tights around her toes. She was wearing a heavily woven cream skirt and a matching jacket, which covered a cream, silk-like blouse. Around her neck hung a string of pearls. Her face was unusually smooth for somebody of her age, helped by the amount of powder she had obviously applied. Her lips were thin and coloured in the same shade as the sofa. Her grey hair was set neatly. She would have passed for twenty years younger than she was, which Ian knew from his research was ninety-six. She smiled.

"Hello, Ian, how are you?" she said gently. Her attire had made him expect her to speak in the Queen's English, but her voice was sharper: short, snippy bursts, fast and to the point.

"I'm very well," Ian said. "And you?"

"Oh, I'm fine," she said, nodding. She was looking out of the window.

"Do you, er, remember me?" Ian said. For a moment, he was concerned that her original greeting had simply been her repeating his name from when the deep-voiced man introduced him.

"Of course," she said, continuing her stare into the sky.

"I'm—"

"I said I remembered, dear," she interrupted. "You're Paul's son. My grandson."

"That's right," he said.

"It's been more years than I care to remember, though," she said. "Your niece's funeral, I'd suggest."

Ian was pleased. He hadn't known what to expect when he had finally confirmed that his grandmother was alive and in the nursing home. For all he knew, Louisa may have lost mental capacity years earlier. He'd half-expected to be greeted by a withered and deaf old woman who didn't have the first idea who he was – who couldn't remember her family or, worse still, even her own name. But the lady in front of him, his grandmother, was anything but that. She seemed very bright, her memory intact. And it suddenly struck Ian that she was likely to hold the answers to his questions.

He edged forward in his seat.

THIRTY-FIVE

Where the hell was he?

It was now early afternoon. Rachel had tried ringing Ian's mobile on several occasions but it was switched off.

She tried again.

Voicemail.

It was pointless leaving yet another message.

She had spent the morning wandering between the kitchen and the lounge. Each time she thought she heard the sound of a vehicle, she had leapt up and rushed through the hall to look out of the window. Each time she was greeted by nothing but the tree mocking her. She imagined the bark on its trunk forming into the shape of a mouth and laughing heartily at her.

She remembered the previous summer, when the nightmare first began.

Ian stood back from the tree, blocking the blazing sun with his hand. God, it was hot. In fact, it was more than hot. Sweat dripped from his body. He collected his bottle of beer from the pathway and took a long drink and burped. The treehouse looked fantastic. Growing up, his father had told Ian on numerous occasions that he was useless at manual work. It was, apparently, something that should be left to Stuart. Not that Dad ever gave Ian the opportunity to get involved.

Standing here today, looking up at his construction high up in the tree, he could categorically confirm that his father was wrong. For a moment, he wished Dad was here to see it, but he quickly dispelled that thought. Immediately, he could hear his father's disapproving monotone voice picking out each and every fault in Ian's work, telling him the way that he should have built it. With all this in mind, Ian was doubly impressed with how it had turned out.

It had taken Ian the best part of the week to build. He had spent hours researching the project, buying the correct wood and following the plans that someone on the internet had helpfully shared with the world. And now it was finished. Wooden stairs ran around three sides of the tree, each side getting gradually higher until the stairs reached a platform near the trunk at the lower branches. Attached to the trunk was a wooden ladder, which stretched up just under two metres to another platform. This platform was larger than the others and easily had space on it for two adults. Ian had built it on the only branch that pointed in the direction of the house. The thickest of all the branches selected especially for this purpose.

The platform was surrounded by a waist-high balustrade on three sides. On the fourth side was the treehouse. Ian had just finished applying the final coat of red paint to the door on the front: the final piece of the plan. Inside the treehouse there were two rooms. The first was large enough to fit a small table in the middle. Ian had placed five cushions around the table for Harry and his friends to sit on. Through the back of the 'dining room' was a further room. It was smaller than the first, but easily large enough for two children to lay down their sleeping bags and camp out for the night. This wouldn't happen for several years yet, though – maybe when Harry was seven or eight.

Rachel had protested when Ian had come up with the idea of building the treehouse that Harry was a little young. But she did concede that it may just brighten up the overwhelming darkness of the tree. And that was exactly what it did. The clean, fresh wood gave the tree a new, almost friendlier look. The treehouse, peeping out from the upper branches, made the view from the cottage far less threatening, much warmer.

Ian took another drink from his beer and pushed open the front door of the cottage. He called Rachel's name and she appeared in the kitchen doorway. She had a finger on her lips and was frowning slightly. She looked up at the ceiling. Ian covered his mouth with his hand, silently apologising that he hadn't considered that Harry was upstairs. Nap time. Rachel smiled and pointed at Ian's beer. Ian nodded and went back outside.

He was joined a few moments later by Rachel and another ice-cold beer. She looked beautiful. She was wearing a short lemon vest, small denim shorts and sandals. Her skin was tanned from the week they had spent together in the garden. A week away from work, together as a family. Ian had wanted the treehouse to be a surprise, but it hadn't been possible. It was more than unfair to ask Rachel to spend the entire week indoors missing the sunshine just so Ian could do a 'grand reveal' when it was complete. Instead, whilst he had measured and cut the wood, she had pottered around the garden, tidying up the flowerbeds and planting new life in place of the brown sticks that poked from last year's plant pots. After nursery, Harry had played in the garden around them, offering his help to Ian when the mood took him.

Rachel stood alongside Ian and they both stared up at the tree, shielding their eyes from the sun. He noticed she was nodding. This was a good sign. She put her arm around his shoulders, causing him to flinch. His skin was reddened by the sun. It was sore, but no amount of pain was going to stop him until the task was complete.

"Sorry," she said, moving her arm away.

"It's okay." He smiled. "Just a bit sore."

"God, they are," she said, standing on her tiptoes to look at his shoulders. She took his beer and had a sip.

"So..." he said, nodding toward the tree.

"It's not bad, I suppose." She giggled. Her face shone. For a second, Ian wondered how he had managed to be with someone so pretty.

"Not bad?"

"Yeah, not bad." She kissed him on the cheek. "Are you going to show me around?"

"Of course, Mrs Perkins. Follow me."

THIRTY-SIX

As the conversation developed, Ian began to feel more and more guilty. His grandmother – Louisa, she insisted – confirmed that she hadn't had a visitor for nearing twenty years. She had moved into the home when her second husband, Alan, had died. She passed Ian a photograph from the coffee table next to her. Ian nodded. He remembered Alan from the funeral. He had worn a purple waistcoat.

All this time Louisa had been alone in this same room, effectively waiting for death to swoop in one day and take her to where she believed she would meet Alan again. She didn't care to speak about Ian's father. As far as she was concerned, he died the moment he forced her from the cottage. She was happy for Ian to speak about his research and she tried to be as helpful as she could. From time to time, he would pull out a document or photograph from his folder and ask her to confirm his understanding of a situation or family relationship.

He felt like a fraud, sitting there in *her* room drinking *her* tea, probing her for information – effectively interrogating her for his own gain. Not once did she complain. It appeared that in some ways she had been prepared for his visit and she had intimated that she sensed his arrival. He apologised on numerous occasions for not coming to visit her before now, and each time she replied with a smile and a shake of her head. She told him: she had known that one day he would come.

"You will be having lunch with me, won't you?" she asked. It was more of an instruction than a question.

Ian was in two minds. He had promised Rachel that he wouldn't be long and whatever conversation was awaiting him at home had seemed extremely serious. On the other hand, he still had numerous questions to ask and getting to the bottom of the curse was more important. Whatever it was that Rachel had to say, it would simply have to wait.

Ian helped Louisa up from the chair and she linked her arm with his as they made their way to the table. He pulled out her chair and she slowly sat down. It seemed appropriate for Louisa to be at the head of the table, Ian to her left. There was a knock at the door and the deep-voiced man pushed in a small trolley. He placed a small silver salver in front of each of them, nodded and left.

"Go on then," she said, nodding toward the salver in front of Ian. He lifted the lid and placed it on the trolley.

"I do hope you like salmon," she said, removing her lid.

"I do, it's my favourite," Ian said.

"I thought so," she said. "I ordered it yesterday especially."

As they ate, Louisa continued to share information about the family. She told Ian of her first husband's tragic death. Ian had read many articles about his grandfather's accident, and Louisa confirmed that the details of the tractor incident were as the newspapers had reported.

Ian wanted to move the conversation along. Louisa had made

it clear that she wasn't happy to speak about Dad. However, neither had she mentioned Uncle Stephen. Ian needed to know the truth about that hot summer's day when Uncle Stephen came to visit and was never seen alive again. He chewed a mouthful of asparagus, considering how to broach the subject of the death of her youngest son.

Louisa eyed him carefully. "You can ask me," she said.

Ian's chewing slowed and he swallowed, making room for some words. "What about?"

"About Stephen," she said frankly.

"How did you know?"

"Well, it's obvious, dear. It must be part of your research."

"It is. But I don't mind if you don't want to talk about it," Ian lied.

"No," she said, her eyes suddenly brightening, "I'm more than happy to talk about Stephen."

Louisa explained to Ian everything there was to know about his uncle. She described him as a playful, mischievous boy. A boy who had a smile that "seemed to bring the sunshine out". He had been too young to know his father, who died while he was still a baby. She told of a boy that was obsessed from a young age with motorcycles. "In fact," she corrected herself, "he was obsessed with anything with an engine." She told Ian about a motorcycle accident when Stephen was fourteen that left him with a permanent limp. He had shown little interest in the farm, leaving that to his brother, Paul. From his early teens, it seemed Stephen had grand ideas of leaving the area and seeing the world.

Following the incident involving Ian's father that effectively forced them out of Cobweb Cottage, Stephen had lived with Louisa and Alan. After that he had gone to university – "the first in the family," she proudly stated. Ian had always been told that he had this accolade. Stephen was always a pleasure to be around, she said, and the three of them would play endless card games into the night and talk about the world.

He was sensitive, caring and loving. "Maybe a little too much in some quarters," she said, winking. "He had more girlfriends than the length of my arm." When he finished university, Stephen achieved his dream of travelling, spending "three or so" years away.

Louisa placed the final forkful of cold salmon into her mouth. Ian rested his chin on his fists and waited for her to begin speaking again. For the first time since he arrived that day, the room fell dark. The sun had taken cover behind a cloud, seemingly too fearful to hear what she was about to say.

She placed her cutlery down on her plate and looked at Ian.

"Stephen was finally settling down." She sighed. "He had a good job and a nice girlfriend. It was all falling into place. And then..."

Ian waited.

"You'd be too young to remember him, I suppose."

"I remember him coming around one day. I was maybe eight."

"*That* day," she corrected sternly. "He only ever came around

261

that day, and he never came back."

Ian moved his hands to his lap and bowed his head slightly. He somehow felt guilt for what was about to come.

"I asked him not to go to the cottage, but he wouldn't listen."

She moved her cutlery slightly closer together. Perfecting the parallel.

"He went over to see your father to make amends. After what happened, Alan and I didn't want anything to do with Paul anymore. Nothing."

Ian understood why.

"But Stephen, well, he was high on life, I suppose, and he drove over there to bury the hatchet. You know, let bygones be bygones."

Tears welled in her eyes. Ian wanted to reach across and hold her. Something stopped him.

"And of course, that's what he decided to do. And once he'd made his mind up it was impossible to persuade him otherwise." She smiled sadly. "He said that he'd go over for a chat and sort things out. As you know, he never came home."

Ian thought he knew what had happened next, but he needed to hear it from her.

"He got that car to celebrate getting his new job. An editor at a newspaper. And I warned him about driving too fast."

"What happened?" Ian asked.

"Well, I don't know what was said with your father. But whatever it was, Stephen left in a hurry and…"

She paused to compose herself.

"...he lost control. He was going far too fast. And that was it."

Ian swallowed. He remembered the day vividly. The argument. The gun. The shot. Was it really a car crash? He needed to know.

"Was there a coroner's report?"

It was something he hadn't come across in the piles of paperwork in his study.

"Yes. I went to the hearing. Apparently, Paul fired a gun to scare Stephen away. And it worked. He drove off at such a pace." She dabbed at her eyes with her napkin. "The only blessing was that he died instantly."

"I'm sorry," Ian whispered.

"Let's have a coffee," Louisa said.

Ian nodded. He didn't know how to feel. That was one mystery dealt with. Ticked off his list.

Sadly, there was to be one more difficult question.

THIRTY-SEVEN

Rachel checked the clock again. It was after three now. She was beginning to worry. The anger she'd felt for the last two hours had subsided and now she was more concerned that something terrible had happened to Ian. That he was lying dead somewhere. As she stared out of the kitchen window, she couldn't help but think back to the previous summer.

"Up you come then," Ian said, reaching down his hand.

"It's a bit high," Rachel said.

Ian was standing on the platform outside the door to the treehouse. Rachel stood at the bottom of the ladder, looking up at him. Together, they had made their way up the steps around the tree, and now Ian was keen to show Rachel the house itself.

"Don't be silly," he said, "just up the ladder."

She giggled suggestively. "You just want to get me in the sleeping quarters."

"Absolutely not." He winked.

Rachel put her hands on the ladder and pulled herself up onto the first of six wooden rungs.

"That's right," he said, taking another swig of his beer.

When she reached the top of the ladder he pulled her up and for a moment their bodies touched. He kissed her. He couldn't have loved her any more than he did at that precise moment.

"You first," he said, indicating toward the house.

Rachel got down on her hands and knees. He could see the tattoo on the bottom of her back. He smiled. "Watch the door," he said. "The paint's still wet."

She turned and smiled. He watched as she shuffled through the door and inside. They tried to fit into the sleeping quarters together, but the room was just too small for two adults. Rachel could squeeze in if she lay on her back and bent her knees. Unfortunately, Ian couldn't get through the door without trampling on her. They tried various positions, but eventually decided that it was too much effort in the stifling heat. So they had retreated into the 'dining room' area of the house. The table now separated them. It was clear that the construction of the treehouse didn't cater for two adults laying alongside one another.

Rachel laughed. "It's a design fault."

"No way," said Ian, smiling, "it wasn't built for your filthy mind."

They craned their necks around the end of the table and just managed to touch lips. Even that was an effort. They both slumped back into position. Despite the shade of the branches, it was unbearably hot in the treehouse.

"What do you think?" said Ian.

"I think it's awesome."

"Really?"

"Yeah, seriously. It's a really cool treehouse."

"It's not just a treehouse," Ian said, "it's a you-and-me

265

house."

Rachel smiled. "Aw. It's brilliant."

"Thanks." It meant a lot.

Rachel began to shuffle awkwardly back toward the red door.

"Leaving already?"

"Yep," she said. "I'd better check on Harry."

Half an hour later, the family of three were together in the front garden. Ian had been out to the barn at the back and collected three deckchairs that hung from a large metal hook on the wall. They must have been left behind when Gillian moved out. The sun continued its relentless assault as Ian struggled to hold Harry down to apply his sun cream. He was taking great delight in slipping through his father's grasp and racing around the front garden. In the end, it turned into a game, Ian 'accidentally' letting him struggle free, and Rachel chasing him around the tree to capture him. The garden was filled with Harry's excitable laughter. Eventually, they calmed him down and told him the importance of covering up in the sun. He had reluctantly agreed to wear his red sun hat, a T-shirt and shorts. Rachel spread out a blanket and brought out ice cream from the freezer. Now, Harry sat looking inquisitively at the house, an orange lolly melting in his hand.

"So it's my house?" he said.

"Yeah, it's yours," Ian said. He finished a beer and opened another.

"So I have to live up there?" He looked concerned.

"No, silly," said Rachel, "it's to play in."

"So I don't sleep there?" Harry confirmed. "Because I like it in my house."

He pointed at the cottage behind him with the lolly. The end fell off.

Rachel laughed and got to her feet. She collected Harry's empty cup and went inside to fill it with fresh water. Ian lay out on the grass, resting on his elbow.

Harry scowled. "It's not funny, Mummy."

"No, Harry, Daddy made it for you and your friends to play in," Ian coaxed.

"Which friends?"

"Any of your friends. It's for when you're older."

"Can I pick which friends? 'Cos I don't like Angelique. She's mean."

"Yeah, sure." Ian laughed, aware of the bully from nursery. "You get to pick who goes in it."

"Oh, okay. That's good then. I think. Isn't it?"

"Yes, that's good, Harry."

Harry moved his head from side to side, smiling. He seemed content with Ian's response and pushed the rest of his lolly into his mouth. He didn't seem to notice that half of it had disappeared. Ian lay on his back and finished his beer. It was going down very well.

Harry stood up and walked over to the flowerbeds.

"Can I water these?" he said.

Ian rolled over to face him. "Yeah, sure. Hang on."

He got up and filled a bucket full of water. Then he showed Harry how to dip his small plastic watering can into the bucket and fill it up. Harry smiled and told Ian that he was going to water every flower in the garden.

Ian watched for a moment as Harry began emptying the first can onto the little yellow flowers. Harry turned.

"I can do it, Daddy."

"I know." Ian laughed.

"So, don't watch then," Harry said.

"Hey, you," said Ian as he entered the kitchen.

Rachel turned from the sink.

"Hi," Rachel said, raising her eyebrows. She dropped two ice cubes into Harry's cup and secured the lid. She placed it on the work surface.

"Just come for another bottle," Ian said. He shook the bottle to show it was empty and then put it on the side.

She grabbed his hand, then put her hand around his waist. "Are you sure you don't want anything else?" she said and pulled his waist into hers.

Ian feigned escape. "No, just a beer."

She stood on her tiptoes and kissed him. He put his arms around her waist and pushed his hand up her vest. Her back was slightly wet, and he stroked her soft skin as they kissed. She pulled away slightly and moved her head to his ear.

"I love you so much," she whispered.

"You're only after me because of my treehouse skills," he said.

She pushed her hands around his waist, bending her arms so each hand held the muscles at the top of his back. They kissed again. He fed his hand down the back of her shorts and squeezed her. They continued to kiss, until Ian slid his hand around the side of her hip.

"Ah-ah," she said, shaking her head. She pulled away and playfully wagged her finger in front of him. "That'll have to wait until later."

Ian leaned in for another kiss and she pecked him.

"Now get your beer," she said. "Oh, and can you take Harry his bottle? He needs hydration. I just need to nip to the loo."

"Sure," Ian said, "get ready for later..."

Rachel smiled. Ian heard the toilet lock click into place. He opened the fridge and collected a beer, then stumbled slightly and overcorrected himself against the work surface. It must have been the combination of heat and alcohol. He stood at the sink for a moment to focus before beginning his journey outside. He stared across the fields, taking in the beauty of his surroundings. It had never looked like this when he was younger. The open sky, the background of the rolling fields, the fresh green lawn leading from the stone wall at the end of the garden to just outside the window where he was standing.

As it always did, his mind quickly switched to the reason that he was standing there. And as his mind switched focus, so too did his eyes, drawn directly to the side of the barn outside.

It was showered in sunlight and it was already possible to see small bunches of white grapes hanging from the vines that weaved from one side to another. And then, his mind took him through the wall and inside the barn. Where it was dark and cold.

To where Stuart had been and to the reason that Ian was standing there at that precise moment.

The click of the toilet lock distracted him, instantly bringing him back to the kitchen.

"Are you still in here?" Rachel said.

"Er, yeah, just going outside now."

"Has Harry had a drink?"

"Not yet, no. Sorry."

Rachel rolled her eyes and smiled. A kind of I-can't-trust-you-to-do-anything-but-I-love-you-regardless look. She took the cup from the side. "You coming?"

"Yep," he said.

They walked together down the hall into the garden.

THIRTY-EIGHT

The deep-voiced man seemed to know exactly when dinner was over. There was a light knock on the door and he entered, pushing the same trolley. On it were two cups of coffee, the steam rising and then getting lost on its way to the ceiling.

The man insisted on helping Louisa from the dining table back to the lounge. Ian carried the two mugs over and placed Louisa's on the small coffee table next to where she was sitting. Alongside the photo of Alan. Ian nursed his cup, and they both waited in silence until the man had cleared the dinner plates away.

The door clicked behind him.

"Are you okay?" Ian asked, taking a sip of his coffee.

"Yes," Louisa said, making herself comfortable in her chair. "Why?"

Ian shuffled forward and perched on the edge of the sofa – so close, he could have touched Louisa if he had wanted to.

"I just wondered, you know, after…" He nodded toward where they had just eaten.

"That conversation? Yes, of course I'm fine, dear. Are you?"

"Yes. I just don't want to upset you, that's all."

"Don't worry about that, I'm a tough old bird," she said, smiling. "And anyway, you have more questions."

"How do you know that?" Ian asked.

"Well, you wouldn't still be here if you hadn't."

The comment caught Ian off guard. He couldn't work out if there was something deeper beneath the statement. It seemed slightly barbed. He didn't know her well enough to know whether her tone had a hint of sarcasm. Louisa must have picked up on this, because she said:

"Don't take offence, dear. You've been a poor grandson, but equally I've been a poor grandmother. Let's agree on that. Then we can move on."

Ian nodded. She was right. It was true that he had made no attempt to contact her until this desperate time of need, but likewise she had never contacted him either. To the best of his knowledge they had only ever met twice before, each time at a funeral. She must have known that had she been so inclined she would have been able to find him easily enough. Some member of the Perkins family would always be in residence at the cottage. Until this moment he had stuck to his pledge that he would never have anything to do with the family. And that was his reason for not getting in contact: a promise to himself.

He wasn't sure what Louisa's reasons were for not making contact, but whatever they were, the fact remained that she hadn't tried to get in contact either. And that was why they were now in this position.

Ian felt a little less guilty now.

"I made a promise too," she said. Her eyes had drifted toward the window again. Ian was unsure what those five words meant. She seemed to understand his confusion.

She swallowed.

"And poor Stuart," she said. From a small drawer in the coffee table, she pulled out a photograph and passed it to Ian. He remembered the day well. The day he left for university. He and his brother outside the cottage.

"It's a shame about the sun," she said.

Ian took a closer look at the picture. He could see a faint smile on his own face. Stuart's face was obscured from the shoulders up. A reflection of the sun, perhaps from a vehicle on the drive.

She continued: "Such an unhappy life. Trapped on that farm. I must say, though, that I didn't expect that."

"Expect what?"

"The gun, dear." She turned to him. "Shooting himself."

"How do you know about that?" Ian asked.

"What do you mean?"

"Well, how do you know about Stuart? You know, if you've not been in contact with anyone?"

She smiled and looked directly into his eyes. It was a comforting smile. "The little boy told me, of course."

Ian frowned.

"You're going to ask me now, aren't you?" she said.

Ian nodded slowly. "Is it true?"

"I think so," said Louisa. She reached out her hand and placed it on top of his. It was warm. Ian felt a single tear fall down his cheek. He was overwhelmed with relief. He knew it. It was true. He was right.

"He's in there, isn't he?" she said, nodding to the folder.

Ian reached into the folder. In a small brown envelope toward the back were the photographs. He pulled the envelope from the folder and passed it to Louisa. She reached inside and took out the pictures. There were no more than ten. Ian watched her face as she studied each photograph one by one. She maintained a friendly smile throughout until she got to the last one. Ian could see the faded writing on the back.

"Here he is," she said. She turned the photograph to Ian. "He's the one who began all of this."

Ian interrupted, his voice quickening: "One by one they've died, haven't they? Right from George Perkins – all the way down the generations."

She nodded.

"In every generation since George. I'm right, aren't I?"

"Right about what?"

"There's a curse, isn't there? Started by George." Ian was trying to hide his excitement. He knew he was almost there. "In each generation one of the children has died before the parents. That's right, isn't it? Is it?"

"Yes, dear. Always the first born."

"I knew it. I'm right. Stuart died before my mother. Uncle Stephen died before you. In fact, the curse took my dad before you as well."

"And it goes on," she said.

"All the way up to George, who started this with the tree and the dog, and –"

"That's right."

Time went by. Ian showed Louisa all the remaining papers in his folder. She studied the family tree carefully, completing a few missing names from the late nineteenth century. They made no difference to the overall conclusion, but Ian was pleased to insert them all the same. A couple of tiny pieces from the edge of a ten-thousand-piece jigsaw puzzle. He wrote them neatly on the paper. Louisa offered anecdotes and stories about his ancestors.

The pivotal point was that they both agreed without question that the curse was real. And that was what Ian had hoped to hear.

It couldn't just be coincidence that one by one children had died before their parents. Ian was happy to concede that perhaps a few hundred years ago, when little was known about diseases and sanitation and hygiene, children would die before their parents. But the curse didn't stop there. It continued on and on, sweeping through the generations, bringing sadness and sorrow on each family, cruelly arriving and taking the first-born child and leaving the parents behind, their lives shattered. Each generation that passed brought about another funeral. Another casket. Another wave of everlasting grief.

He knew he was right.

He knew that he wasn't to blame.

He needed to get back to Rachel to tell her everything.

To get back to where they were before.

Louisa finished her coffee.

"I'm getting tired, dear," she said.

Ian checked his watch. It was ten past five.

"Okay," he said. He pushed the papers into his folder and clipped it shut. He stood. "Thank you so much," he said.

"Thank you for coming," she said.

It didn't seem appropriate to hug her, so Ian stood over her for a moment before tapping her hand gently. "I'll be back to see you again," he said.

She smiled.

"Let's not make any promises," she said.

THIRTY-NINE

Ian carried a beer in one hand and Harry's cup in the other. Rachel linked arms with him as they walked down the hallway.

The first thing that Ian saw as he reached the front door was the brightness of the sun, burning with an intensity that he had never experienced before. The sun seemed to be concentrating its rays directly through the front door of Cobweb Cottage. As a reaction, both he and Rachel covered their eyes with their forearms and paused for a second, allowing their eyes to adjust to the sudden darkness. The light was so bright, so intense, that it hurt. It was as if the sun was sending a special message just for them, a light as bright as burning magnesium to get them to avert their eyes – if only for a second. To save them.

The second thing that Ian saw was the small body lying on the grass at the foot of the tree.

FORTY

Ian accelerated along the country lane. He was conscious he was driving a little bit too fast, and his mind quickly switched to Uncle Stephen. He pressed the brake and watched the needle reduce back down to the speed limit. This was no time to repeat history and feed the curse. But he couldn't wait to get home. He felt like a pioneer who had spent his entire life researching a vaccination or creating some feat of engineering, something that would change the world, and he'd finally found that it worked, the lifetime of research had paid off. This was his eureka moment. What he had found out would change the world – at least his and Rachel's world. Without his noticing, the needle crept back up.

He reached down to the passenger seat and flipped his phone over. The screen told him he'd missed eleven calls, all from Rachel. He had seen them as he pulled shut the large red door of the nursing home and walked across the gravel car park. He'd very nearly rung Rachel at that moment, but decided that he would do so on the journey home. He was too eager to get moving. It seemed better to call when he knew that the distance between them was shortening with each sentence spoken. And now, as he checked his phone for what seemed like the millionth time since he set off, there was still no signal.

Eleven missed calls. That was a lot. In a way, Ian felt quite pleased. It was the most attention he had received from her for months. He knew it didn't really bode well, though. He was in no doubt that she was worried about him. He had only intended to pop out for two or three hours, no longer than that, and now the daylight was fading and he was still just under an hour away from home.

As the trees and hedgerows rushed past him, he decided to use the remaining time in the car to prepare himself for what Rachel was going to say. The difficulty was knowing what it would be. It was likely that she was either going to suggest that they separate or get some help for their relationship. It had to be something life-changing. He was sure that's what she said as he was leaving earlier that day.

The suggestion of a separation or, God forbid, a divorce would be the worst possible outcome. Surely she couldn't suggest that. All those years before, they had both committed that they would "never be like everyone else". True, they were young and naïve then, and true, they couldn't possibly have known what life had in store for them. But that was the commitment they had made and Ian was sure that they'd both meant it. Surely Rachel wouldn't go back on this now and suggest that they separate. Surely not.

He pushed his foot down and took the car smoothly around a tractor.

He had to admit that he wasn't sure. He and Rachel had shared so much silence recently that he had no idea what was happening inside her head. He knew that his love for her was just as strong as it always had been. It just felt different; almost incomplete. Like they were on either side of a glass screen unable to touch one another, unable to share how they felt. It was too painful, too desperate, to show it. He just hoped that she felt the same. He pictured the palms of their hands pushing together, separated by an inch of transparency. If she rejected his love, he may as well climb the sycamore tree as well. If Rachel suggested they part then, he decided at that moment, he'd use the emergency hammer, obliterate the glass and release everything. He had nothing to lose.

The green and yellow fields were swallowed by scattered barns and buildings, which soon became a small market town. As he slowed behind a queue of traffic his phone beeped twice. A signal. The village bustled with activity as people headed to take the last bus home. They carried shopping bags and weaved in and out of the stationary cars. The traffic crept forward. Every so often a driver would seize their opportunity to escape and accelerate a few metres forward, to get into the gap between them and the car in front without killing a pedestrian.

Ian felt around on the seat for the phone, keeping his right hand on the wheel. An endless trail of elderly shoppers continued to cross the road, lifting their bags to squeeze through the narrow gaps between the cars.

There were two further missed calls, both from Rachel. That was thirteen in total. He noticed that he had one bar of signal and swiped the screen to return the call. He lifted the phone to his ear and edged the car forward again, narrowly avoiding a tartan shopping trolley. Rachel answered immediately.

"Where are you, Ian?" Her voice was angry, probably diluted slightly with worry.

"I'm, er, just on my way through –"

"What?"

"I said" – he spoke more slowly – "I'm just on my way through –"

"I can't hear you. It's just crackling, like static."

Ian glanced at the screen. Still one bar.

"I said that –"

"It's no good," she said, "you'll have to call me back."

The line went dead. Ian pressed the red icon on the phone to end the call. He tried to redial, but the one bar had disappeared.

Ian was back on the open road, the market town now far behind him. He had tried numerous times to get through to Rachel again without any luck and had decided that he would leave the conversation until he got home. He glanced at the clock – it couldn't be more than twenty minutes now. His thoughts turned to the only other reason he could think of that Rachel needed to speak to him so desperately.

Counselling.

A therapist.

Medication.

Or something like that.

He knew from the magazines she read that therapy was the answer to most of their readers' problems. Sometimes when Rachel left in the morning to take Harry to nursery, Ian flicked through the problem pages and read the letters that people sent in, seeking advice. He found some small comfort in reading about other people's problems. It made him feel...well, less alone. It seemed from the magazines that a therapist was almost a fashion accessory nowadays. Phone, purse, watch, therapist. This seemed especially true across the Atlantic. Well, he thought, if this was what Rachel wanted to talk about then he was happy to go along with it. There was no harm in trying.

The road suddenly climbed above everything around it. The fields and streams dropped dramatically away on either side to create an elevated spine rising from the earth and cutting through the landscape.

It suddenly struck Ian that none of this was going to matter anyway. Whatever it was that Rachel so urgently needed to say to him would change when she heard what he had to say. He smiled. It was funny, because everything had changed and Rachel *didn't even know it*. He imagined that she had been pacing the house all day, practising what she wanted to say to him, repeating her dialogue over and over. And all along, none of it was going to matter.

Not at all.

He shook his head and jokingly cursed himself for bothering to even waste time thinking about this stuff. He had solved the riddle of the family and brought closure to the subject once and for all. He pushed his foot down as the fields rose up to meet the road. He couldn't wait to get home and tell Rachel everything.

About Louisa. About the tree and the dog and the curse and how nothing was his fault.

Nothing.

It was all destiny.

He could never have done anything to stop it.

It was written long before he had even been born.

Before Rachel had been born.

Before Harry.

It was all predetermined.

They had all played their roles to perfection.

It had happened just like it should.

Just as the curse had wanted.

FORTY-ONE

Ian's ears were ringing. The only sound he could hear was screaming. Ear-piercing, endless screaming.

As Rachel drew breath her throat vibrated violently, as if the noise was tearing and stripping the skin inside.

Ian raced over to where Harry lay and threw himself to the ground alongside him. He could see blood gathering on the grass beneath Harry's hair. He turned and screamed at Rachel to call an ambulance. She ran inside the house.

Harry's eyes were closed and Ian could see a large, triangular opening in the top of his skull. The area was wet and shiny, fresh blood pumping slowly like lava from the wound. Ian lowered his head and put his ear to Harry's mouth. He couldn't hear a sound, the screams had made his hearing fuzzy, but he was sure he felt a faint breath. He didn't know what to do next. Everything he had read or seen told him not to move Harry. To leave him where he was.

He had to stop the bleeding.

He got to his feet.

Rachel came running from the house. "Is he breathing?" she screamed.

Ian looked around. Behind him on the picnic blanket was

Harry's red hat. He picked it up and scrambled onto his knees, holding the hat tightly against Harry's head. The blood quickly soaked into the hat, dampening his fingers. Through the hat, he could feel the fragments of Harry's skull moving between his fingers. He screamed at Rachel to get something else for him to use. She left again and returned with a T-shirt from inside the house.

"Oh-my-God-oh-my-God-oh-my-God-oh-my-God-oh-my-God-oh-my-God-oh-my-God-oh-my-God-oh-my-God-oh-my-God-oh-my-God-oh-my-God-oh-my-God-oh-my-God," she repeated breathlessly.

She folded the T-shirt into a square and passed it to Ian.

He removed the hat and replaced it with the T-shirt. Blood soaked his hands. His forearms.

And then Rachel was on her knees, her ear to Harry's mouth.

"He's not breathing," she screamed.

"Jesus," Ian said. "Move him onto his back. Come on."

Ian held the T-shirt to Harry's head and together they moved him onto his back. Blood spilled out from his throat, drowning his lips.

"Hold this," said Ian, nodding toward the T-shirt. Rachel put her hands over the moist fabric and held it down.

"Don't push too hard," said Ian.

And now he was directly facing Harry, using both his hands to gently prise his mouth open. He reached his fingers inside and pulled Harry's tongue to the side and began to breathe into his tiny mouth. Long, deep breaths.

And then he had his hands on his son's chest, pushing firmly, careful not to go straight through his ribcage. And then the breaths again.

And the pushing.

And the breaths.

Rachel began to scream again. Ian couldn't hear anything. He felt the heat tearing into his neck and back. Everything was hazy. He wasn't really there. The colours became brighter. Into focus. And then all other colours faded and there were only two.

The red of the blood.

The green of the grass.

The breaths.

The pushing.

He looked up at Rachel. Her mouth was open wide, her face blurred and contorted. He looked along her arms to her hands. Everything was red. The T-shirt was wet. Dark.

And then he felt a hand on his shoulder, gently pulling him backwards, and he was standing. By the trunk of the sycamore tree. Watching.

It was only then that he properly saw the position in which his son lay. Only then that he saw his leg crudely folded beneath his body, snapped upwards beneath his back. Twisted. Like the branches of the tree, snapped.

A female paramedic was trying to move Rachel so she and her partners could get closer to Harry. Rachel was on all fours, as if she was looking for something on the ground. Her hair fell down one side. He could see her face, bloodied and red. Her mouth was still open, saliva elastically attached to her mouth, dripping toward the ground.

A man was breathing into Harry's mouth, whilst another unwrapped a plastic mask. Ian heard no sound. Nothing. Everything was moving so slowly. The mask was over Harry's face now, held in position. The two men glanced at one another. One stroked the hair away from Harry's forehead.

Ian knew it was too late.

Far too late.

The figures disappeared into outlines of where they used to be. Deep red splashes against the bright green background.

He steadied himself against the tree.

And he was sure he heard a voice.

No more than a whisper.

"Leave me here. Always," it said.

And then everything came into focus again. Screams filled the air; the woman was holding Rachel back. The men were lifting Harry onto a stretcher. He looked tiny against the white background.

He didn't move.

FORTY-TWO

Rachel was waiting at the window as the car finally came into view. Ian was driving much faster than usual.

The black metallic paint flashed between the white fence posts at the end of the garden. The branches of the sycamore tree leaned curiously in the direction of the car.

She was angry that he had taken so long to return.

The car slowed slightly and then swerved into the driveway. It stopped abruptly a few metres from the front door. She watched, trying to get a first glimpse of his face. That would tell her a lot about how the conversation was going to go.

Ian jumped out of the car and waved. A broad smile was pinned to his face.

She lifted her hand slightly and then quickly drew it away. She didn't feel like waving to him.

As he approached the front door, she saw she had misinterpreted his smile. It was more a grin. A stupid grin.

The door opened and slammed shut.

"I'm back," he almost sang. "You'll never guess what I found out today."

She swallowed hard and walked into the hall.

"Where have you been?"

"I've been visiting family."

"Right," she said warily.

"Yeah, sorry I took so long." Ian put his folder down on the floor and sat on the stairs. He posted a finger inside his trainer and slipped his foot out. He looked up at her. "It's been one tiring day."

"Ian, we need to talk."

He pulled off his other trainer and tossed them both against the skirting board. "Okay," he said. "Let's get a coffee first. Yeah?"

Rachel thought for a moment. "Yeah, okay," she said.

FORTY-THREE

"So," Rachel said. After a full day of practising her speech, she had hoped to do better than stumble after one solitary word.

They were sitting in the kitchen, Rachel at the end of the table, Ian in his usual spot, with the view of the garden and the wall and, somewhere in the distance, the stream that trickled endlessly by, oblivious to what was happening. Ian asked Rachel to wait a moment while he organised all his papers. He took them from the folder one by one and placed them precisely on the table. The photographs. The family tree, complete with the red crosses. His notebook. Lined A4 sheets with his scribbled handwriting.

She watched patiently as he moved them around in front of him. Soon, the kitchen reminded her of a police incident room. When he seemed satisfied that he had everything just the way he wanted it, he looked up.

"Before you start," he said, "I just want you to know –"

"Ian," Rachel said gently, "stop."

She had waited all day for this and she wasn't going to be railroaded. She wasn't going to listen to what he had to say until she had spoken. As far as she was concerned, this was their last chance.

"We need to talk. Because I need you to know some things."

He was watching her carefully, certain she was about to cry.

He hoped not – there was no need; she'd be happy once he had told her everything.

"Ian, before I say what I'm going to say, I want you to know that I love you. Okay?"

He nodded. His mouth twitched.

"I mean that. I really do love you, and –"

"Rachel," he interrupted, "I need to tell you something."

"No, Ian. You need to listen –"

"But what it is will change everything. I swear –"

"No. You'll listen to me," she said firmly. The words reminded Ian of the way she used to speak to Harry.

"But –"

"Ian. No."

Ian couldn't take his eyes off her. He loved the way that her mouth formed words, the almost invisible smile that she permanently wore – a slight upturn of her mouth at each side that, if you looked carefully, was always there. He was disappointed that she hadn't let him speak first. To tell her about the curse. He watched her, but couldn't focus on exactly what she was saying. His mind was filled with names and dates and funerals and trees and curses. From time to time, he would hear a sentence or two, but then the words would fade and he would be left with his brain telling him not to forget to tell her about what had happened to this person. How this person had died. How he had worked out each clue. His research. This photo. That diary.

He moved the papers with his hand. Her voice came back.

"For God's sake, Ian, leave those papers alone. Are you even listening?"

She seemed angry now. She didn't let him answer.

"This whole research thing needs to stop. Right now. This family tree bullshit, it needs to stop. Our son, *your* son, is dead."

"But –"

If she'd just let him speak, he could explain.

"No, Ian. Your son is dead. We cremated him. Remember?"

He stood up.

"Sit down. I'm not finished."

He sat back down on the seat. He wasn't sure where he was going anyway.

"Harry is dead, Ian. That's it. We, you," she corrected, "have to deal with that. You need help. Proper help."

"But –"

"No! You need help. It can't go on. *I* can't go on."

She was crying.

"Rachel," he said quietly. "Listen to me. There is a curse, okay?"

"Oh, for Christ's sake, Ian."

He reached for the family tree on the table. Exhibit A.

"Listen. Please. The tree is cursed. It controls the cottage. The people in it."

She was watching him now. She seemed to be listening. Her face was slightly contorted. She looked like she had tasted something bitter.

"It started years ago. Centuries."

He lifted the picture of George Perkins. In the photograph, he had an angry look on his face. He was standing just beneath the tree, his family around him. The reflection of the sunlight obscured the face of one of the children. Exhibit B.

"This is George..." Ian said.

Rachel was shaking her head. Tears rolled down her face. Her cheeks shone.

"Many years ago –"

There was the sound of a chair scraping against the floor. Rachel stood. "I'm sorry. I can't listen to this," she said.

"Rachel, it's all true. Louisa confirmed it."

"Louisa?"

"Yeah," he said, "today. That's where I've been."

He held up the compliments slip from the nursing home. Exhibit C.

Her face broke again and she left the room. A moment later she returned with a small black handset. Ian recognised it from the shelf in the hall, where it usually sat redundant in its cradle. She slid it across the table to him. It spun as it got closer, and he quickly guarded his papers with his forearm. He looked at her suspiciously.

"Listen to the message," she instructed quietly.

Ian frowned.

"Listen," she said.

Ian pushed the button with the little picture of an envelope on it. There was a brief beep. Then a voice. Female. It told him that there was one new message, received that morning at nine thirty-six.

There was another beep and then a voice. One that Ian recognised. A deep male voice. It spoke clearly, without emotion. The speaker must have said words similar a hundred times before.

"This is a message for Mr Perkins. I'm calling from Tall Trees Nursing Home. We are sorry to inform you that your grandmother passed away in her sleep last night. Perhaps you'd be kind enough to give us a call."

The message ended and all that was left in the kitchen was a long, monotonous tone coming from the phone in the centre of the table.

Rachel walked to where Ian was sitting and reached for the phone. She pushed the button and it was silent.

She took Ian's head into her hands and pulled him close, into her chest. Stroking her fingers through his hair, she whispered to him that it would all be okay. In the end.

He was numb. Physically numb. And although in that moment he didn't know exactly how he felt, he did know that he was ready for everything to be stripped away. For the wooden walls he had built around himself to be pulled down. And for the first time in front of Rachel it felt right to let the tears flow. Tears that had been locked behind the glass for far too long.

And in the front garden, the tree swayed and rustled in the wind as a wall of thin rain fell, separating it from the cottage.

For now.

About the author

M Jonathan Lee was born in Yorkshire, England where he still lives to this day.

When not writing, you'll find him standing at the back door thinking.

His first novel, *The Radio* was nationally shortlisted in the Novel Prize 2012. *Broken Branches* is his fourth novel.

Acknowledgements

Thanks to the crop of people who watered the seed that grew into *Broken Branches*:

Charlie Wilson, Nick Jones, Terry Brookes, Matt Niblock, Stephen Lee and Sarah Catley.

HIDEAWAY FALL

web: www.hideawayfall.com
twitter: @hideawayfall
facebook: /hideawayfall